Blind Ambition

Blind Ambition

A Novel

Douglas F. Greer, M.D.

iUniverse.com, Inc.
San Jose New York Lincoln Shanghai

Blind Ambition

Published by iUniverse.com, Inc.

For information address:
iUniverse.com, Inc.
5220 S 16th, Ste. 200
Lincoln, NE 68512
www.iuniverse.com

ISBN: 0-595-15111-6

Chapter *One*

March

Pamela Wilcox grabbed the car phone and began dialing 911. Suddenly the sign to the Lincoln Tunnel appeared. She hurled the phone aside. She cut the wheel hard to make the turn, and, looking again in the rear view mirror, was certain she saw the white van drive straight ahead and disappear into the pre-dawn blackness. She exhaled slowly and murmured a prayer. It must have been her imagination.

From the moment she'd pulled out of her garden apartment building a half hour earlier, she had the sickening feeling of being followed. Twice she had spotted the white delivery van weaving in and out of traffic 50 yards back. It was when she turned her head and saw the van right on her tail that she panicked.

Thirty-five-years old and still paranoid, Pamela thought. She patted the sealed manila envelope lying on the passenger seat. It was going to hit like dynamite, she whispered to herself. Her brother would have been proud. She paid the toll and maneuvered her blue Ford Bronco into one of the lanes for the tunnel. Again she looked back. No sign of the van.

In the tunnel she zipped by a lumbering cement truck, slowed to cruising speed, read the time on the dash clock. 5:04 am. Smart to get started so early, she figured. Beat the rush hour traffic. When she reached Metrocare Hospital, she would have plenty of time for breakfast before meeting the doctor. Maybe she'd stop into one of the new gentrified establishments on Ninth Avenue for Eggs Benedict, her favorite. No, bad idea. She'd lost four pounds, and was determined to lose the remaining nine.

She primped her dark brown bangs in the rear view mirror and frowned at her coke-bottle glasses. It wasn't her fault, she thought. She'd wanted to wear her contacts, but the old ones were too coated and dry, and the new ones she'd ordered hadn't arrived. Oh, well. She wasn't driving to Manhattan for a modeling audition. Still, she hated the specs. She assessed her freshly-painted fingernails. They looked just fine.

When she reached the hospital it was still dark. She drove around the oversized city block twice before spotting the hospital's parking garage on Ninth. Once through the electronic gate, she drove down the ramp to a lower level, expecting it would have an underground tunnel to the hospital just like the one where she worked.

Turning off the ramp, she noticed that the level was empty but for a few unoccupied vehicles. She looked for a sign to a tunnel. She found none. Again fear gripped her, but ebbed when she sighted the faded red arrow to "elevators" on the other side of the garage. She swung into the first empty space to her right, killed the engine, rammed on the emergency brake.

Pamela pulled down the sun visor, flipped up its illuminated mirror, and discovered that, in the morning rush, she'd forgotten to put on her eye makeup. She opened her glove compartment, found her spare makeup bag, and took out the eye shadow applicator. She removed her thick glasses, placed them on the passenger seat beside the manila envelope, and leaned within inches of the mirror to bring her eyelids into focus.

Sensing a motion to her right, she was at first confused. Hadn't a bare arm reached through the passenger window and quickly vanished? She whirled in her seat, her vision a blur. She groped for her glasses, accidentally knocking the manila envelope beneath the seat. The glasses were gone.

Terror replaced confusion, and she screamed, throwing open the door. She bolted from her car. Without the glasses, the garage was a dark blur. She smashed headlong into the side of a parked van. Blood spurted from a gash in her forehead. She screamed again and ran, sobbing and panting. She tripped over a coil of construction cable, pitched to her knees and, gasping, struggled upright.

It was then that the muscular arm caught her from behind. A hand slapped a sheet of duck tape over her mouth, gagging her screams. For a split-second she raged with the realization that, of all things, the near-sightedness had brought her even to this, half-blind in a dark parking garage when only sight could save her. She reached back and dug the nails of both hands with all remaining strength into the attacker's scalp. She heard a grunt of pain. The arm tightened further around her neck, and the last thing Pamela Wilcox saw was the flash of the knife that swooped downwards plunging into her heart.

CHAPTER *Two*

The eye was what caught Jack Stegall's attention.

Not that the homeless old man staggering across 9th Avenue didn't stand out otherwise. With his double-tassled pink stocking cap, florescent orange "I Love New York" sweatshirt, rainbow-colored tights, and purple jug of cheap wine, he looked like a drunken harlequin wandering off course.

But just as he passed in front of Jack's car, the old man squinted with his left eye in a way Jack immediately recognized. Without a doubt the cornea had been injured. And when the old man almost dropped his cane to use his hand to shield the eye from the just-risen Manhattan sun, it became obvious the trauma was recent.

Straining forward in his seat, Jack stared at the peculiar eye until the traffic light turned green. The line of trucks and cars behind him began to inch forward, but Jack kept his foot on the brake to let the inebriated man cross safely. The fusillade of honking horns and screaming drivers was instantaneous.

"Go! Drive, asshole!" shouted the truckdriver directly behind, leaning out the window of his cab. "Move it!"

Jack defiantly held his position until the old man reached the curb. Then he shifted into low, drove across 53rd, and made an immediate left into the doctor's entrance to the parking garage directly across 9th from

Metrocare Hospital. Activating the electronic gate with his plastic card, he drove into the shadowy interior, turned right, and coasted to his assigned parking space. In the middle of the space, the roughly stenciled white lettering shone in his headlights: "STEGALL, M.D.—EYE."

Jack parked and checked his watch: 6:23 a.m. and right on schedule. Ninety minutes to pick up the preserved human eye tissue at the Hospital Eye Bank before heading to the operating room for the corneal transplant.

He started to adjust the rear view mirror to assess his appearance, but stopped, preferring not to know if the lack of sleep showed. If he had seen his reflection he would have detected no outward signs of fatigue, just a slim face framed with dark brown hair, with thick lashed, alert blue eyes. One would have guessed him to be a well-rested man five years younger than his actual age of thirty nine. Only a few lines above the brow and a faint fullness of the lower eyelids betrayed the greater wear and tear.

Jack loosened his tie, carefully pried the lid from his coffee, took a sip and relaxed in his seat to prepare himself mentally for eye surgery. Glancing through the windshield, he had an unobstructed view across 9th Avenue to Metro-care. Scanning the multiple facades of the fifteen story, city-block hospital complex, he pictured the sequence of operative maneuvers he would use for the case. Reaching for his coffee, he carelessly bumped the cup into the emergency brake lever. The hot, black decaf sloshed across his worn Samsonite briefcase, barely missing his taupe suede sport jacket and freshly pressed gabardines.

"Damn!" He hastily set the cup on the dash, grabbed some tissues from the glove compartment, and soaked up the spill. Looking down, he saw the coffee spot on his tie. He smacked the steeling wheel with his hand in fury.

Knuckles rapped on the window. It was a blue-uniformed hospital security guard.

Jack cracked the window. "Yes, it's OK—just coffee."

"Sure, doc?" The guard beamed his flashlight through the windshield onto the empty passenger seat.

"No problem." Jack was embarrassed. The irritability had been coming on for months. Small things would annoy him, people would get on his nerves, so much so that even an old habit—digging his right thumbnail into the flesh of his index finger when he was tense—had resurfaced. Was it his breaking up with Sarah? Or had he just been working too hard?

"All right, doc." The guard snapped off the flashlight and turned to go.

Jack noticed the revolver on his hip. They usually weren't armed. "Officer. I've never seen security over here. What's up?"

The guard pointed off to his left. "Woman murdered on Friday. Stabbed to death."

"Right here in the garage?"

The guard nodded solemnly.

"Who was she?"

"Not a clue. No car, no keys, no purse, no glasses, no nothin'. She was found yesterday in the back of a stolen van." His pager beeped. "Watch out for the construction, doc," he said, pointing across the street. "There's bricks and dust flying everywhere." He strode off dialing into his cellular phone.

Great place to come back to, Jack thought. One unidentified murdered woman, and, by the way, watch out for the falling bricks. He looked across the street and spotted the construction at the hospital's massive, arched entrance. Workmen in hard hats were taking down the old granite letters of the hospital's previous name, Mercy Hospital, and installing huge new brass letters.

"There it goes," Jack said beneath his breath. Like so many New York City hospitals, Mercy was in the red. A national hospital chain had bought Mercy and renamed it Metrocare as part of their aggressive marketing plan. Jack had interned at Mercy, and the new name seemed a violation. He lowered his gaze from the busy workmen to the small, shady park situated between the front of the hospital and 9th Avenue. The name "Mercy Park" was still wrought in the rusting iron arch spanning across its stone-pillared entrance. At least that survived, Jack thought.

He rechecked his watch. Six-thirty three and time to get moving. Gulping the remains of his coffee, he emerged from his car when a brand-new green XJS Jaguar coupe pulled into the adjacent space marked "Matthews, M.D.—Neurosurgery." Through the windshield the two doctors exchanged perfunctory waves. The car came to a halt and Dr. Frederick Matthews got out. A short, stout, balding man in his mid-fifties, Matthews wore a light blue seersucker suit tightly stretched over a protuberant abdomen. His beefy facial features were set in the usual scowl.

"Morning, Matthews. New wheels?" offered Jack, locking the door to his 1989 silver-grey Porsche coupe.

"Yeah," answered Matthews, peering up at Jack's athletic six foot one frame. "And it cost enough." The stodgy brain surgeon extricated a Gold Pfeil leather briefcase from the Jaguar's back seat, slammed the door, and patted the shiny rear fender. "Stock market," he smiled.

Matthews walked a few paces ahead of Jack, talking backwards over his shoulder. "What time do you have, Stegall?"

"6:30."

Matthews accelerated. "Damn. Late."

Matthews' antsy behavior amused Jack. Wherever the brain specialist was, there always seemed somewhere else he was late getting to. Not so amusing, however, was that Matthews' impatient habits were spilling over into the operating room, where he was even rushing during his brain surgery cases. Whether Matthew's impatience was some compulsive quirk, or was the result of trying to make more money faster, no one was sure. But already people were calling him "Fast Fred" behind his back.

Stepping from the shadowy garage into the bright New York sunlight, both men waited at the curb for the traffic to clear. To their left, a homeless woman foraged in a city waste can. Matthews sneered, "Jesus, Skid Row is getting worse around here."

"Mercy Park," Jack said, referring to the scores of homeless people who had drifted there to survive the winter. Peering across the avenue beyond the park's fence and shrubbery, Jack saw outlines of the improvised huts, lean-tos, broken beach umbrellas, and tents. Blue smoke threaded through the trees from a solitary fire somewhere amidst the shelters.

Matthews continued walking, speaking more to the gutter than to Jack. "More uninsured people who don't pay. My malpractice premium just went up to $90,000 a year."

When the two men crossed the street, Matthews, now ahead by several paces, turned northwards to avoid the park. Jack hesitated, realizing if he cut through the park he'd not only reach the hospital faster, but could ditch his annoying colleague.

Surprising even himself, Jack chose the unpopular path.

"Gotta run. See ya," he said.

Matthews responded with an unintelligible grunt and continued on, indifferent to Jack's vanishing.

Jack passed between the park's tall iron gates and, flanked left and right by the sleeping forms of the vagrants, jogged across to the hospital entrance. Taking the hospital steps two at a time, he passed through the tall, glass double doors and headed for the Eye Bank.

CHAPTER *Three*

120 West 70th Street
6:36 a.m.

Gabrielle Richards' bedside radio came on just as the WHTZ DJ was cueing in over the fade of John Lennon's "Imagine." With one blind jab, Gabe hit the snooze button and buried her face back in the pillow.

In the next bedroom, Gabe's roommate, Maria Sanchez, already up practicing her karate, heard Gabe silence the radio. Maria paused to make one more attempt to deliver her roundhouse heel-kick to the ski-masked face of the inflatable dummy bobbing in front of her. With jet black hair flying and muscles straining beneath her lycra shorts and sweat-stained teeshirt, she missed her target badly, lost her balance, and crashed to the floor. Cursing softly, she grabbed a towel, wiped the sweat from her glasses, and walked to Gabe's bedroom door.

"Attention, all 4th year medical students," announced Maria. "This is your dean speaking. Anyone caught still asleep will be required to repeat their proctology rotation." She emphasized her slight Hispanic accent to make the bit funnier.

Gabe didn't budge.

"C'mon, Gabe, no second snoozer today," Maria said, toweling her brow. "Don't want to be late to Metrocare the first day."

"Ohmigod! Surgical specialties," gasped Gabe, jerking her head up from her pillow.

"We're due at 7:30," Maria said, turning down the hall towards the bathroom.

Pushing wisps of wavy, dark brown hair from her eyes, Gabe groped on the night table for her glasses. Squinting, she could see only hazy outlines of the tortoise shell spectacles resting at the table's far edge. Fumbling, she overshot her mark, and the glasses skidded across the table towards her. Before she could catch them, they fell to the floor and bounced under the bed. Shifting her teeshirt-clad body crossways to the bed for balance, Gabe put both hands on the floor and dropped her head below the bedframe to see under, raising one leg for balance. Maria, walking past the doorway back to her bedroom, noticed Gabe's unusual semi-handstand.

"Yoga?" Maria inquired.

"Blindness," grunted Gabe, using one hand to hold the cascading strands of hair from her eyes.

Gabe's upside-down view revealed her elusive spectacles, still out of focus, but now also completely beyond her reach.

"Great, just great," muttered Gabe. Forced to get out of bed and get down on her hands and knees, she extended her arm fully and snared the glasses. She stood up, put them on, and her medical student apartment instantly came into focus—desk, surgery books, chair, pathology books, computer, internal medicine books, bed, more books. Also Maria, watching from the doorway.

"This week is karate class, Gabe, remember? You said you'd help me with my heelkick."

"OK, but let's make it fast."

In Maria's bedroom, Maria repeated the attempt at a roundhouse kick. This time her glasses went flying across the room as she failed more miserably than before.

"The key to the spinning kakato-geri, Maria, is balance and follow through," Gabe said, taking position a few feet in front of the dummy.

"No, Gabe, do the whole thing, you know, with the stepping reverse punches."

"Gyaku-zuki? OK, if you want." Gabe walked back several paces, turned, and assumed the starting position of "kamae"—feet spread, fists at her side—and stared at the dummy. Her smile was gone, replaced with a look of deadly intent. She sprang forward, sequencing three stepping reverse punch movements, fists rocketing forward, to bring her within range of the dummy enemy, then crouched, whirled, and violently struck the dummy square in the face with her right heel, simultaneously grunting, "Mugger!" The concussive impact almost toppled the dummy and sent its ski-mask hurtling through the air onto Maria's textbook-cluttered desk.

Maria stood transfixed as the dummy continued to bob wildly from the deft blow. "Incredible! Gabe Richards, you absolutely disgust me. Is there anything you can't do?"

"Nothing," laughed Gabe, replacing the mask on the dummy's head.

Maria swung on her bathrobe. "First dibbies on the shower!" she sang out heading for the hallway to the bathroom.

"There you go, first again. Hey, don't take too long! I've gotta shave my legs!" Gabe yelled. She gave the dummy a final playful flick with her index finger, and walked back to her room.

Gabe slipped into a robe, crossed to the window, and looked through the blinds down the eight stories to West 70th Street. A few shafts of sunlight licked across the sidewalk and apartment buildings on the north side of the street opposite her. A solitary garbage truck rumbled by, heading east towards Columbus Avenue. She raised the blinds and cracked open a side window. The air was clear and smelled fresh. She closed her eyes and inhaled and exhaled deeply, as if drinking in the beginning of what promised to be an unusually challenging day, the first day of the surgical specialties rotation at Metrocare Hospital. For four weeks they would be introduced to ophthalmology, hand surgery, neurosurgery, plastic surgery, narrow disciplines which up to now had been practically omitted from their medical education.

Gabe strode to the bathroom. There the steam from the shower instantly fogged up her glasses. She removed them, popped open her contact lens case, and delicately scooped out the clear soft lens with the tip of the index finger. Lifting her right upper lid, she touched the glimmering wet shell of soft plastic onto her right cornea.

Her shower finished, Maria reached outside the stall for her white terry cloth bathrobe and saw Gabe putting the other contact in. "That reminds me, Gabe, I'm gonna put mine in, too."

"How are the new ones doing?"

"Not much better than the previous pair, damn it. My eyes still get red and uncomfortable. It's a drag."

Squeezing past each other, Gabe entered the shower stall, and Maria went to the sink where she opened her own contact case and removed the right lens. It immediately slipped from her fingertip and fell into the sink basin, where it became indistinguishable from adjacent droplets of water. Leaning over, she bumped her head on the faucet twice before she was able to identify the lens and fetch it out.

"Gotcha, you little bugger," she muttered, rinsing it with saline and starting all over. Her technique was clumsy compared to Gabe's.

"Gabe," Maria complained, raising her voice loudly enough to be heard over the shower. "What's your secret with these things?"

"I don't know," shouted Gabe as she lathered herself with soap. "Been at it for years. They're like part of me. You only started with contacts last year, Maria. And you don't wear them all the time. Don't give up. If thirty million other Americans can wear them, so can you."

"Yeah, well, I think they're a bummer, and the only thing that's worse is glasses," said Maria.

"Hey, welcome to the club. I hate glasses, too," said Gabe.

"Gabe, you don't understand. I'd do anything to get rid of glasses. I would kill, I would maim…" A sudden recollection brightened Maria's face. "Ohmigod, Gabe, I completely forgot to tell you. One of Metroc-are's eye surgeons does a new operation for nearsightedness. You know, it was in Time Magazine, the one we just got."

"Get real. We're in medical school. Who has time to read magazines?" replied Gabe, who had reduced the flow of the water to shave her legs. "Wait—you mean that operation the Russians invented, radial cornea or something—you know, the one where the patients are on this assembly line circular conveyor belt, and the surgeons make the little cuts with…" she dangled her razor out over the shower door for Maria to see, "…razor blades?"

"Gross! No, that's radial keratotomy, the one that they found out makes you farsighted," Maria sang out. "This is something new, really accurate. According to the Time article, it makes radial keratotomy look like something out of the dark ages."

"Oh. OK, then how does this new gizmo work?"

"Well, they use a new laser called a Free Electron Photonizer," answered Maria, who was now struggling to get in her second contact lens. "It zaps your eyes—actually the center of your corneas— for about ten seconds and—presto!—your myopia disappears."

"Oh, you must mean the excimer laser operation," said Gabe, her halfshaven left leg now propped up on the small plastic stool in the corner of the shower.

"No, the excimer laser can cause distortions and ruin your night vision. The Free Electron thing uses a vacuum and runs off a linear accelerator. The whole thing is called Free Electron Refractive Keratectomy, but they use the acronym, FERK. It really sounds neat."

"I'm sure it'll be neat for the doctors who have the machine."

"How so?"

Gabe started shaving her other leg. "Isn't something like 25 percent of the world's population nearsighted? Can you imagine the money doctors would make? Billions. And how do they know it really works?"

"The initial surgical trials worked," Maria shouted back.

Still attempting to put in her other contact, she managed to blink it out of her eye onto her cheek.

Gabe, bathrobed and stepping out of the shower stall, saw the myope-in-distress. "Don't give up, kiddo, you'll get the hang of it." Gabe towelled her hair vigorously. "Try to wear them more often."

"Yeah. Red, irritated eyes and all," complained Maria. "Gabe. What if we looked into getting our eyes zapped when we're down at Metrocare?" With her contact lens finally in place, Maria leaned close to the mirror to check her lashes. "The Time article said they're looking for volunteer patients for the first round of operations."

Instantly Gabe stopped towelling her hair and looked up at Maria. "You're not serious?"

Maria folded her arms and faced Gabe squarely. "Yes, I am serious. I mean, sure, we'll check it out first. But just think. No contacts, and no, ugh, glasses." Maria picked up her glasses and suspended them as if holding a dead rat by the tail.

Gabe looked at her watch. "Ohmigod! We're going to be late!" It's already five to seven!"

CHAPTER *Four*

"Human Eyes. Refrigerate. Do Not Freeze."

The words, in bold red lettering, were printed on stickers plastered on all four sides of the foot-square styrofoam box Jack had claimed at the Hospital Eye Bank and now held under his arm. As he approached the elevators, he did his best to conceal the lettering. He was used to carrying a box of refrigerated human eyeballs around like a lunchpail, but he knew the uninitiated would not share his point of view.

Jack moved quickly to the elevator, which opened as if on cue. Inside, he pressed the button for seven. Just before the doors closed, a hand caught them, they reopened, and more people jostled in, including two female medical students, who immediately pored over their assignment sheets. Both women were obscured until everyone else got off on the second floor. Jack was about to look at the two students when Dr. Matthews stepped on, carrying several thick neurosurgery charts.

"Hello, again," said Jack, wishing he'd taken the other elevator.

"Stegall," returned Matthews flatly.

The pair of students, still absorbed in their reading, continued to ignore their two fellow passengers.

The elevator stopped on the third floor, admitting a chubby lab technician slightly out of breath and pulling a small cart loaded with blood tubes and blood-drawing paraphernalia. She edged directly to the back, pushing one student closer to

Matthews, the other closer to Jack.

"Had a great case last night," the brain surgeon said, looking at Jack. "This woman came in comatose. Had a cerebral cystic hemangioma the size of a grapefruit." "Got it out in less than twenty-five minutes. Fun case."

The two students raised their eyebrows. The one closest to Jack turned towards him. Returning her glance, Jack studied the face for the first time.

Gabe Richards smiled, forcing Jack to look away and conceal his feeling of absolute vulnerability. A moment later he glanced back. He couldn't stop looking at her. It's the combination, he thought—good looks and an intelligent face. The explanation felt right, but failed to stop the rush.

Gabe looked back at him, with an even broader smile, which Jack this time returned. Then, with effort, he redirected his gaze elsewhere.

At the sixth floor a technician wheeled her cart away and a group of tired-looking general surgery residents replaced her.

When the elevator reached seven, the operating room floor, everyone exited, the residents heading purposefully to the right. Jack, Gabe, and Maria stepped off last. When the two women hesitated, Jack saw his opening.

"Looking for the main corridor of the OR?" he asked, trying to read Gabe's name tag. "It's down to the right. You'll see the double doors on your left." Before he could make out her name, both women had thanked him and were turning down the corridor. He watched Gabe until she rounded the corner and disappeared. He had the urge to chase after her, find out her name, not let her get away. But he checked his watch, and realized that he would already be late.

He turned to the left and entered the OR floor through a pair of heavily scuffed double doors marked "Housekeeping—Operating

Room—Do Not Enter." By using the little known short cut, he might still get there on time.

The women zigzagged around patient-laden stretchers and ducked IV poles to reach the group. Before they had a chance to exchange greetings, a short, unsmiling nurse appeared from the OR office. "Surgical specialties elective, fourth year medicine," she announced. There was no traditional white uniform, no white at all. Instead, she wore a green business suit, well-tailored, pressed, with a beige ascot tucked beneath her neck. A gold lapel pin read "Metrocare OR."

The students fell silent, motionless, as the middle-aged woman studied them over halfcut reading glasses perched on the tip of her nose. Behind the glasses, heavy layers of black mascara accentuated a chalky complexion. Her hair at the back was perfectly rolled up into a French twist.

The nurse produced a roster from her pocket and took attendance. All nine of the senior medical students were present.

"I'm Miss Craig, OR nurse supervisor," she continued. "Usually the senior surgery resident supervises your elective, but he's out sick, so I'm in charge. This rotation lasts four weeks. Be here no later than 7:30 every morning. If you are late, you are absent that day."

"Can you believe her?" Maria whispered when Miss Craig looked up to synchronize her wrist watch with the corridor clock.

"Your duty is to shadow your assigned surgeon," Miss Craig went on. "Sometimes you will just watch, sometimes you will be asked to gown up and scrub in to assist. Each week you will be assigned to a different surgeon, four weeks, four surgeons in all. Wherever he or she goes, you go—surgery, office visits, emergency room, conferences, whatever."

One of the students wisecracked, "Golf at the Club?"

The supervisor stifled the giggles with a stern glare. "One exception to your assignment. Every day at 11:30 you are required to attend your lecture on surgical specialties in the SCT, the Surgical Conference Theatre located down the corridor. Be there, and be prompt. Now, here are the cardinal rules in surgery: Follow strict sterile procedure, don't get in the way, and most of all, be on time. Punctuality is a prerequisite here at the Metrocare OR. Every surgical case begins at 8:00 a.m. on the dot. We are punctual. We expect you to be."

She tapped her wrist watch with an index finger, and quickly checked its time with the wallclock again before continuing. "When I give you your individual assignment, you can go to change into your scrubs and report to the indicated operating room. Here are your assignments. Starting with Abramowitz, you'll be in Operating Room 2, plastic surgery, beginning with a mammoplasty, Dr. Brice will be your surgeon. Next, Chen, Room 3, hand surgery, carpal tunnel release, Dr. Deaver, surgeon; Hamilton, Room 5, neurosurgery, that begins with a laminectomy, Dr. Herz, surgeon: Richards, Room 13, eye surgery, cataract extraction and artificial lens implant, Dr. Royster, surgeon; Sanchez, Room 14, eye surgery, corneal transplant, Dr. Stegall, surgeon…"

When Miss Craig was through, Maria spoke up. "Excuse me. Our instruction sheet says we can switch assignments with each other."

"That's correct, but if you swap with one of your fellow students, it sticks for the remainder of the week." Craig turned and walked off.

"Gabe, you got Royster!" Maria exclaimed, eyes brimming with excitement.

"Right, I got Royster," Gabe replied, puzzled.

"Royster! He's the one I told you about!" Maria whispered loudly, looking about as if there was some secret to keep.

"You mean the doctor with the new ..?"

"Yes! FERK! Free Electron Refractive Keratectomy," Maria replied as the twosome walked towards the women's surgical locker women. "Gabe! Would it make that much difference to you if we—I mean—switched? I mean, I've been so interested in this stuff. Anyway, I'm assigned to an eye surgeon, so you'll get to see eye surgery anyway. What do you say?"

Gabe looked up into Maria's pleading brown eyes. "Well, it's a super opportunity, Maria. But I guess you discovered it, after all. OK. I'll swap."

"You're a pal. I'll to go tell Craig."

"Wait, who's my guy again?" asked Gabe.

"Stegall, Room 14."

"Oh, yeah, Stegall. And he's doing a corneal transplant, about which I know zip. You've been boning up on this corneal stuff, Maria. Make me an expert in 20 seconds."

"I've only read up about the FERK," Maria said. "Oh, that reminds me. Here's the Time Magazine with the article about FERK." She extracted it from her tote bag, flipped to the dog-eared page, and handed it to Gabe. "See?"

"I hadn't expected a full page article." Gabe read the title aloud, "New York City's Metrocare to be Myopia Mecca," then sat on a bench and continued to read silently:

"Last week, New York City's Metrocare Hospital announced that its new laser operation, FERK, which eliminates myopia in seconds, will soon be offered to regular myopic patients. With 25 percent of the world nearsighted, ophthalmologists' waiting rooms may soon be overflowing with patients wanting the procedure…"

"Can you believe it?" uttered Gabe.

"Keep it to finish later," Maria sang out as she headed down the corridor to find Miss Craig.

Gabe found the women's surgical locker room, changed into scrub clothes, mask, and cap, and headed straight for Suite 14. There the sign on the door read, "Corneal transplant microsurgery in progress. Absolute quiet please." She glanced at the video monitor perched above the scrub basin outside the suite. It read "Corneal Transplant, 8:00 am. Attending Surgeon: Jack Stegall, M.D."

Gabe approached the door. It's small window was a little higher than usual, requiring her to crane her neck slightly and touch her mask to the glass to peer through.

Inside, the operating room was almost completely dark, except for one vertical shaft of white light which seemed sus-
pended mid-air in the middle of the room. Gabe blinked and pressed closer to the glass. The eerie lightbeam streamed downwards from a ceiling-supported operating microscope onto the right eye of the anesthetized patient lying supine on the operating table. Sterile sheets covered the patient's entire body except for the eye, which was held wide open with a silver-wire, spring-loaded lid spreader. To the left of the patient's head sat the instrument nurse. Directly behind the patient sat the surgeon, gazing through the binoculars of the surgical microscope, his figure silhouetted by the solitary shaft of light.

"And this must be Stegall," Gabe whispered to herself.

CHAPTER *Five*

"Cut!"

At Jack's command, the instrument nurse reached across the eye-drape with the microscissors to the patient's exposed eye. Avoiding the eyeball itself, she cut the ends of the suture Jack had just tied. Fullsize, the microscissors were two inches long. But in Jack's magnified view through the binocular surgical microscope, they were the size of hedge clippers. The eyelashes were as big as baseball bats, the fine black nylon sutures as wide as electrical cable, the pupil a giant hole, and the eyeball itself a great cyclops filling Jack's retinas entirely.

Jack had just begun the operation, and had ordered the overhead lights turned off to accentuate the retro-illumination from the surgical microscope. So far, he was pleased with the surgery's progress. The prepping, draping, and positioning of the eye had gone well. There had been no problems with the induction of general anesthesia. An experienced team of nurses had been assigned to the operation. The microscope was functioning perfectly, there was the reassuring, biofeedback-like steady beep of the Okidata heart monitor, and, he thought, there were no more distractions—no garage murders, no Matthews, and no beautiful women riding elevators.

Just then, the circulating nurse, noticing Gabe looking in at the window, walked to the door and nudged it ajar. "You're the medical student assigned to Dr. Stegall?"

Gabe nodded and retightened the strings on her mask in preparation to enter.

"Dr. Stegall is just beginning the case," the nurse said in a West Indian lilt. "Wait here for a moment." The nurse closed the door gently and moved silently through the semidarkness to the operating room table. "Dr. Stegall, your medical student assignee is waiting outside. Shall I bring her in?"

Jack nodded.

The nurse opened the door just wide enough to allow Gabe to slip inside, joining the darkness. Taking her arm gently, the nurse guided her a few steps along the tile wall to the right. "I'm Cissy Walker, the circulator," she whispered. "Stand here a few minutes until your eyes adjust to the dark."

Cissy Brown stepped forward and whispered in Jack's ear, "Dr. Stegall, do you want the student to just observe the video monitors, or watch directly through your second observation scope?"

"The scope's the best," he said in a hushed voice. "In a second we'll move her in. What's her name?"

Cissy removed a list from her scrub shirt pocket and checked it with her penlight. "Maria Sanchez, doctor."

"Welcome, Sanchez," Jack said into the darkness.

"Good morning, doctor. I'm Gabe Richards. We switched assignments. Maria requested Dr. Royster."

"Welcome, Richards," said Jack, concealing his annoyance as he introduced his assisting nurses. "Cissy, position our student at the observation binoculars."

Cissy placed a surgeon's stool in front of the second pair of binocular viewers to Jack's right, and gestured to Gabe to sit down. "Just place your hands in your lap, sweetheart, and try not to jostle the microscope."

Gabe obeyed. As her eye came up to the microscope's binoculars, she saw the magnified view of the patient's eye.

"My God, I've never seen the eye this closeup," exclaimed Gabe. "It's amazing, it's beautiful!"

Jack didn't look over at Gabe. But the loveliness of her voice made him exquisitely aware of her, her closeness, the rustle of her surgical garb, the faint fragrance of perfume.

"Cissy," Jack ordered, "let's display the microscope view on monitor three now."

Cissy went over to the audiovisual rack, flicked a switch, and the same magnified view of the eye appeared on the second large Sony screen.

From behind a sterile drape on the other side of the operating table came the deep, resonant voice of the anesthesiologist. "Great view from here. Thanks, Jack."

"Oh, I forgot. Richards, you haven't met our anesthesiologist. Gabe Richards, meet Dr. Sam Bankert, the best gasman in the East." Jack meant the compliment. Of all the anesthesiologists he had worked with, Sam Bankert was tops.

Jack looked over to his left to see the anesthesiologist, seated as usual between the patient and the massive anesthesia cart, one hand on the ventilating apparatus, the other jotting notes into the anesthesia record. Dr. Bankert looked up at him, then gave Gabe a short, friendly hand salute. It was a salute in more ways than one. He was wearing a marine combat fatigue cap, instead of the usual blue OR cap. Jack had noticed Dr. Bankert's unusual headcover at the beginning of the case, but had decided to ignore it for the time being.

"Seen eye surgery before, Richards?" asked Jack as he readjusted the eyelid spreader.

"No."

"Well, let's review the anatomy first." Jack took a small pair of forceps to use as a pointer, identifying the white of the eye first. "This, as you know, is the sclera, the tough white part of the eye. The cornea here," he continued, pointing to the round window in the front of the eye, "is the transparent structure through which the light rays enter. It's transparent because its collagen fibers are layered evenly and positioned more or less in phase with light waves. As a result the waves pass through the fibers undisturbed. Now, in our case this morning, the cornea needs replacing. If you look closely here, Richards, you'll see that our patient's cornea is not clear like yours or mine. You see, the cornea has become hazy from scarring."

Gabe seemed to press closer to the oculars of the microscope. "Yes, it is hazy, it looks whitish. But why does it have to be replaced with a transplant?"

"Because clear vision can be affected by even the smallest amount of haze or scarring or irregularity of the cornea," Jack explained, adjusting the clear plastic eye drape. "This cornea is so bad the eye is legally blind."

"If de cornea get hazy, de vision go crazy," Cissy added from the side of the room, giving her West Indian accent added zing.

"Dr. Stegall," Gabe asked as she concentrated through the microscope, "what made this patient's cornea become hazy to begin with?"

"Long story, Richards. Briefly, her cornea deteriorated because she had cataract surgery with the implantation of an intraocular lens." Jack said. "Are you familiar with cataract surgery and implants?"

"I've managed to read up a little," answered Gabe. "As I understand it, a cataract is a clouding of the tiny lens inside the eye behind the pupil, and when it's removed it can be replaced with a tiny plastic lens implant in the space left by the removed lens."

"Very good," Jack smiled. "This patient had cataract removal and an implant ten years ago with an implant imported from Europe that was designed to attach to the edge of the pupil."

"How did that work, with the pupil always dilating and constricting?" questioned Gabe.

"Good question," Jack commended. "In fact…" Jack hesitated. Then he realized the patient was asleep. It was safe to speak candidly. "In fact, it's the very question that was not answered fully before the lens was used in thousands of patients all over the world. It turned out that in a high percentage of cases, the movement of the pupil caused the implant to rub on the iris, causing bleeding and inflammation. This made the cornea scar and become hazy."

Using his forceps, he pointed in the direction of the colored iris. "If you look carefully you can see the little plastic implant itself, and see where it is deforming the edge of the pupil. Here, let me zoom down on it." He depressed the zoom pedal, and in seconds the pupil had tripled in size.

"Oh, yes," said Gabe firmly. "I see it. Are you going to replace it with an implant that works?"

"We could," Jack said, reversing the zoom, "but the patient was so fed up with the corneal complications of the first implant, that she refused. So after this corneal transplant heals, we'll have to fit the eye with a thick soft contact lens to restore the necessary focusing lens power to the eye. It'll be a setback for her, but I can't say I blame her for nixing another implant."

"She must have been so angry when she learned she was given a faulty implant never properly tested," Gabe remarked. "How did she react when you told her?"

Jack found the question distracting. Why, he wasn't certain. Was it because he had in fact not told the patient the truth behind the ill-fated implant? Doubtful. He believed that was not his responsibility. Was he unsettled because he felt vulnerable to the question, even when it came from an apparently naive 4th year medical student who knew little of eye surgery? He wasn't sure, and found himself stumped.

"Interesting question," Jack he muttered to stall for time. His thoughts drifted back to the end of his residency when he'd accepted a position in Washington D.C. with a booming, fashionable eye surgery private practice. There, the highly reputed surgical partners latched on to the new implant lens before it was proven safe. Jack refused to use the untested lens, and saw his own surgical case load plummet.

When the disastrous complication of corneal haze loomed, Jack's fellow eye-surgeons quietly switched away from the offending implants. Nobody told patients what had happened. There was no investigation of the manufacturers, surgeons, hospitals, or medical schools responsible for the implant debacle.

"Shall I open the box of human eyes now, Dr. Stegall?" asked Cissy from the corner of the room.

"Not yet," he answered, absorbed in his thoughts. He had tried hard to co-exist with his zealous surgical associates. But he only became more angry, more unhappy, and his surgical load declined further. Finally, the inevitable: when his associates demanded to know why he wouldn't use the implant, he told them in no uncertain terms that he thought it was wrong. It was only a matter of a few weeks before he was asked to "relocate his practice."

He was fired.

And Jack had learned his lesson: cover your ass.

Jack shifted back on his stool. His thoughts on the subject were now in order, and he felt prepared to answer Gabe's question truthfully but safely. Clearing his throat, he asked for the electric microcautery, then said, "It's a long story, Richards, but to answer your question," he said, confidently sealing a tiny bleeding capillary, "I in fact did not disclose the implant's poor track record to the patient. "Besides," Jack went on, "as in all of these cases, one never knows exactly what may have caused the corneal haze, what other complications may have preceded or occurred at the time of the original surgery."

"Didn't the patient ask about what happened?" asked Gabe, seeming to press slightly.

"No," answered Jack, on the verge of ordering the medical student to be quiet and just watch. "And if the patient had asked, I would have suggested she contact her original surgeon. I'm simply her corneal transplant surgeon."

"Oh," said Gabe. Jack detected the tone of dissatisfaction in her monosyllabic response. Tough. If she wasn't satisfied with his explanation, he was, and put it out of his mind.

Dr. Bankert seemed to pick up on the tension between the surgeon and his student. "How about a little background music, Jack? Want me to turn up the speakers?"

"Not right now, Sam, thanks. Cissy, let's prepare the donor cornea."

Cissy turned up the lights and directed the large overhead saucer-shaped OR light to an adjacent, sterile draped table. Jack and the nurse silently rose, moved to the table, and sat at the two stools on either side.

Cissy went to the box of human eyes, extracted one of two small bottles sandwiched between two refrigerant bags, and loosened the cap. She walked back to Jack's table, removed the cap entirely, and with one careful motion poured the contents into a sterile petri dish resting in the center of the table. At the end of the short stream of pinkish fluid came a small wafer-like disc of tissue, completely transparent except for a small rim of white. It was one of the cadaver corneas.

"Looks excellent," said Jack, scrutinizing the donor corneal tissue floating in the fluid. With a pair of fine corneal forceps, he carefully grasped the bordering rim of sclera and held the disc up at eye level, moving it till it caught the strongest rays of light from the overheads.

As he examined the cornea for clarity and defects, Cissy began to read aloud the accompanying sheet of data. ""Donor—female, mid-thirties. Cause of death—laceration of heart and pulmonary vein secondary to stab wound. Time of death—approximately 6 am, 4 days ago. Lab tests…"

"Wait, Cissy," Jack said. "Did you say the woman was stabbed to death?"

"That's correct, doctor."

"Look at the second page at the bottom. It will tell you where she died."

Cissy flipped the page. "Let's see—location of death was—52nd and Ninth—oh Lord…"

Jack looked over at Gabe. "Amazing. This was the woman who was murdered in the hospital parking garage."

CHAPTER *Six*

"Ohmigod. Who was she?" Gabe asked.

Cissy flipped to the last page. "The Medical Examiner filled this out. Says here she's still a Jane Doe."

"A guard in the garage told me," Jack said. "The murderer didn't leave a clue." He stared at the cadaver cornea. "Wait a minute. Cissy, hand me the portable keratometer."

Cissy fetched the instrument from the wall cabinet, placed a sterile handle, and passed it to Jack. He held it over the cadaver cornea to measure.

"I thought this cornea looked unusually steep. It has 48 units of curve on the front," Jack said. "The victim didn't just have any glasses. She must have been extremely nearsighted."

"And?" Dr. Bankert asked.

Jack handed the instrument back to the nurse. "Without her glasses, she was blind as a bat. If she was without them before she died, she would have been in one big blur."

Gabe gazed at the cornea. "I'm nearsighted. Trust me, if she had a car, she would have needed her glasses to drive."

"Right. But she didn't have them after she was killed," Jack said. He tapped on the dish in which the cornea floated, wondering just what vision of horror passed through her corneas before she died. He glanced over at Gabe. She was also staring at the dish with a shocked look.

"Did you want the Eye Bank's lab tests, doctor?" Cissy asked.

"Oh, of course," said Jack. He had to get back to business.

Cissy read the remaining data, finishing with the eye bank's assessment of the donor cornea prior to its bottling, refrigeration, and delivery. "Clinical appearance. Surface epithelial cells intact, underlying corneal stroma clear, inner endothelial cells appear healthy."

"Perfect tissue for transplantation," Jack concluded. "Just a few days postmortem. If you wait too long," he added for Gabe's benefit, "the inner endothelial cells may begin to die, even under the best storage conditions."

For the next 30 minutes the conversation ceased as Jack completed the meticulous task of excising the patient's clouded cornea and replacing it with the cadaver cornea. When he had placed the first two, critical sutures anchoring the new cornea in place, he felt his muscles relax, his cardiac rate slow. He knew that the crucial part of the operation—transferring the cadaver cornea to the patient without miscutting, damaging, or dropping it—was behind him. That left the simple process of sewing the transplant in with 16 watertight ultrafine black nylon sutures and burying the knots. To prepare the graft for the final suturing, he began to remove the surface epithelial cells with a small scraper.

"I don't understand," said Gabe quizzically. "Won't the graft need those surface cells?"

"Yes, but they grow back from the edges of the cornea postoperatively," he answered. "As long as there is healthy tissue beneath, the epithelium always grows back completely and normally. I'm removing it now because it will only tend to interfere with sewing in the cornea." He handed off the scraper and readjusted the focus.

"So corneal tissue can grow back," recited Gabe.

"No, only the surface cells, Richards. But the tissue beneath it, the actual substance of the cornea called the stroma, won't grow back normally once it has been cut, damaged, or removed. It's just like the skin. Remove some of the skin's surface epidermal cells from a scrape, and they grow back with no scarring. But cut deeper into the dermis, and you get a scar. Same thing with the cornea."

"You mean the same type of scarring and haziness we saw in this patient?" asked Gabe.

Jack zoomed down on the cornea to check the depth of a suture. "Absolutely. Corneal scarring, haziness, and the vision loss that goes with it." Jack began to wonder why she was belaboring the topic.

"But that includes the center of the cornea, right?" she pressed. "I mean, the part that refracts the light rays?" There was now a perplexity in her voice.

"Correct. And your question is?" Jack bit into the cornea with another ultrafine nylon stitch.

"Oh, nothing. It's not relevant right now."

What in the world is bugging this student, Jack wondered to himself.

Bankert broke in. "Anybody want to hear some tunes from MegaMOM?"

"MegaMOM? What's that?" Gabe asked.

Bankert removed his earphones. "The computerized audiovisual system you see all over the OR. MegaMOM stands for MegaMultiOmni-Media System."

"Must have cost a bundle," Gabe said.

"Yeah. Runs on a Hitachi main frame, MVS, extended architecture, the works. Has about a billion megabytes of memory, BAUD rate's out of sight."

He stopped to check the oxygen gauge and made an entry into the anesthesia record. "I got to outfit MegaMOM with music. Loaded the system with hits. Rock, soul, country, you name it. Got all the classical stuff. I even have some cantus firmuses from the Middle Ages." He started to hum what sounded like a Gregorian chant.

"How do you play them?" asked Gabe, still gazing through the microscope.

"You just key whatever you want into the computer," Bankert replied. "The computer communicates with our library of digital recorded music we installed in an old storage room down the hall."

"Sam here has created sort of the world's first operating room computerized digital jukebox," Jack said.

Seconds later the overhead speakers came to life with the sounds of Percy Sledge, "Let me wrap you in my Warm And Tender Love, yeah…"

Jack spotted a loose suture and replaced it. "What was that question, Richards?"

"Dr. Stegall, isn't the new laser procedure—you know, the one they call FERK—an exception to the rule that the corneal tissue always scars when you cut and remove part of it?"

Jack was so instantly thrown by the question, that the movements of his hands stopped immediately, making the microscope's view of the operation look as if it had been freeze-framed. When he went to hand a delicate pair of tying forceps to his assistant, his movements were—for the first time in the case—rushed and jerky, and the 450 dollar instrument fell, glanced off the surgical drape, and hit the floor with a solitary ping.

"Whoops," said the instrument nurse sympathetically.

Cissy kneeled down and retrieved the instrument lying close to Jack's left foot. She stood up and took a close look. The tips were badly bent. "Back to the factory for repair with this one," she announced.

"I'm sorry," said Jack gruffly.

But he wasn't feeling sorry.

He was feeling annoyed, by Gabe, again. Bankert glanced over and saw the frown on Jack's forehead. "I'm sorry? Sure, Jack. Comin' right up." The anesthesiologist tapped on the keyboard and the digital display read "I'm Sorry" -Number one—eight weeks—1960—Decca Records," and the Brenda Lee hit began.

Jack, unamused by Bankert's musical distraction, shot a reproving look at Gabe. Sensing his glare, she returned his gaze. Staring into her hazel-blue eyes, Jack experienced a second, new emotion.

Desire.

Suddenly, helplessly, Jack fell in love with Gabe's eyes.

Feeling confused and vulnerable, he dove back into the view of the microscope. My God, he thought, I've been back in the hospital for less than three hours and I've been lovestruck by two medical students in a row. Christ's sake, get a hold of yourself. Bedroom eyes and surgical camaraderie could make an intoxicating potion.

But he couldn't ignore her vexing remark about Free Electron Refractive Keratectomy.

"Well, Richards, to answer your question about FERK contradicting the traditional belief about corneal scarring, as you know, in about…" Jack glanced up at the wallclock, "…a half an hour I'm lecturing your group, and if you want, I can touch on nearsightedness surgery theory then."

"Theory? But I…"

"But I'll clue you in now. FERK is a very exciting, promising experimental invention, but…" Jack paused to choose precisely the right words, "…let's put it this way. You'll never see the likes of me doing a FERK procedure on any of my patients."

Gabe, her eyebrows knitting together with puzzlement, said nothing. Finally, Cissy broke the awkward silence.

"Maybe none of my business, Dr. Stegall," she offered brightly, "but you wouldn't think that from listening to Dr. Royster. He says the FERK thing is a fantastic medical breakthrough, you know, right up there with the discovery of X-ray, vaccines, MRI, whatever."

"I'm aware of Dr. Royster's spirited enthusiasm for FERK," Jack said flatly. "After all, he has exclusive control over the machine ever since he brought it to the United States."

"From where?" asked Gabe.

"The machine was invented in the United States. A few years ago the Japanese copied it. Then a Dr. Nakamura, an eye surgeon in Tokyo, adapted the machine for eye surgery. After rabbit experiments, he sent a duplicate machine to his Soviet collaborator, Dr. Vorov, an ophthalmologist in St. Petersburg. Vorov refined the technique using monkeys." Jack noticed the corneal graft was drying out. "Let's wet the cornea."

The instrument nurse reached across with a small dropper bottle and applied the needed saline.

"How many monkeys?" asked Gabe.

"Just a few," Jack answered. "Monkey research is expensive. And they were eager to move on to human volunteers."

Cissy, heading for the door with a tray of used instruments, turned around and said, "Yeah, Dr. Stegall, you know the old surgeon's saying about experimental animal laboratory research?"

"What?"

"You know—'One has yet to meet a rabbit who can pay a surgical fee.'" Bumping open the door with her backside, she disappeared into the corridor.

Behind his mask Jack smiled widely as he relished the remark. "So," Jack continued. "Both Nakamura and Vorov formed a company, and sent the latest model of the machine to Royster here in the United States. Somehow Royster rounded up a group of volunteer patients who had small scars on their corneas already. Finally, the Japanese and the Russians approached Royster and some fatcat investors from Germany to buy in. They named it World, no, Globe, that's right, Globe, Incorporated. They're itching to see FERK take off so they can start mass assembling their Free Electron Photonizers abroad and sell them here and all over the world."

"Like China, for example," interjected Gabe.

"China for certain, with their high rate of myopia."

Gabe again remained curiously silent. Jack noticed her reaction, but dismissed it.

"All done here," Jack interrupted, pedaling the foot controls. The microscope slowly withdrew from the operative area, simultaneously moving up and laterally in space, its giant supporting arms jack-knifing together. Jack removed the lid spreader, undraped the eye, and bandaged it. Then Bankert moved in and, with Cissy's help, began to deanesthetize the patient.

"Excellent anesthesia, Sam," said Jack. "Do your magic on the extubation." Jack turned to Gabe to explain. "The less coughing the better with these grafts. There are reports in the literature of grafts that blow loose from postop trauma, including severe bouts of post-extubative coughing."

Suddenly, a loud voice filled the room. Looking up at the central video monitor, everyone saw it was Miss Craig telecasting herself from her office over the MegaMOM system into the operative suite.

"Dr. Bankert, may I please have your attention," Miss Craig said, her pinched face looking directly out of the screen.

Bankert looked up. "Yes, Ms. Craig?"

"Dr. Bankert," Craig said. "I personally video-monitored you during the case. Your surgical cap, whether it is freshly laundered or not, is in violation of the Metrocare OR dress code. And we cannot tolerate the playing of rock and roll dance music. I have assessed two demerit points for your infractions."

"What's my grand total?" asked Sam.

Craig's voice was becoming more clipped. "You have 29 demerits, Dr. Bankert, and I must warn you that if you accrue any more you will be reported to the OR Conduct Committee. Thank you." The screen went blank.

"Sam," said Jack, trying to keep a straight face beneath his mask, "when she came on I thought she was going to nail me for being eight minutes late for my case."

"And steal all the fun from me? Not on your life. I love to yank her chain. I've seen her kind for 25 years of practice, ever since I became a gaspasser. It's great to dish it back."

"Aren't you afraid?" asked Gabe. "Demerits don't sound good."

"I don't have to be afraid of the Miss Craigs anymore or anybody else around this god-forsaken place. You see, I'm short and bare." He paused to listen through his stethoscope to the patient's chest.

"Short and bare?" asked Gabe. "How so?"

Dr. Bankert held his hand up indicating he couldn't hear her. When he removed the stethoscope from his ears, Gabe asked the question again.

"I'm retiring," answered the anesthesiologist.

"And bare?" Gabe prompted.

Bankert lowered his mask, revealing a wide, mischievous grin beneath a graying moustache. "No malpractice insurance. There's nothing to sue me for. Lawyers go for deep pockets. The hospital wanted to throw me out immediately, but they decided to buy a quickie policy to cover their own asses knowing I was leaving."

Jack and Gabe dismounted their stools and, after Cissy untied their gowns in the back, stripped off their surgical gloves, wriggled out of the gowns, removed their masks, and turned to face each other.

"You were in the elevat..," they said in unison as they simultaneously recognized each other, their surprised expressions turning to laughter.

The patient started to moan as she came back to consciousness. Bankert stethoscoped her lungs and re-checked her blood pressure just as Cissy wheeled in the gurney stretcher.

"Thanks, Cissy," said Bankert. "Jack, Richards, give us a hand."

The foursome positioned themselves around the table, and grabbed the corners of the sheets beneath the patient. Bankert gave the order. "OK, when I count three. One, two, three."

In one motion they lifted the patient from the operating room table to the stretcher, and, with Cissy and Gabe holding the double doors to the room open, Jack and Sam slowly wheeled the patient out.

CHAPTER *Seven*

11:09 a.m.

"Keep it professional, strictly business," Jack murmured to himself as he left the recovery unit where he had finished his postoperative routine.

Sure, Gabe was attractive. She was intelligent, warm, down to earth. But she was a medical student and he was her teacher. Besides, she might be only 25 years old, 27 tops. Probably too naive, too idealistic. To act on his feelings would be a major mistake. He would assign her to someone else as soon as possible.

Jack turned the corner and saw Gabe headed his way. She smiled, gave a short wave, but kept her same graceful stride as she neared. The contours of her body offset the linearity of the antiseptic hallway.

"I just finished," he said. "Let's go down to the surgeons' lounge and dictate the case." Great resolutions, he thought.

Jack led Gabe through the surgeons' lounge into the dictation area. The long narrow room lined with cubicles was empty.

"Coffee?" he asked, gesturing to the small serving table in the corner.

Drinks in hand, they sat facing each other. Jack picked up the phone, dialed transcription, and dictated the case in lengthy detail. Finished, he hung up the phone, tossed his surgical cap into the waste basket, and stood to stretch. He could feel the tightness in his lower back. "What do you think of eye surgery, Richards?"

"That was a beautiful operation, very nice." said Gabe. "But I would think you would be on cloud nine," she added, her eyebrows knitting again with skepticism. "Instead, you seem, I don't know, not just routine-minded. You seem kind of—detached. I would think you would feel like you were king of the mountain."

"Right, king of the mountain," he recited, taken aback. He got up and opened the window behind him. A soft April breeze stroked his face. He looked westward over the hospital's buildings and grounds, pretending to take an interest in the view. Gabe was right, he thought, he should feel victorious.

He turned to Gabe and gave her his best answer. "A surgeon doesn't feel like king of the mountain. You'll see that in surgery you develop a sort of detachment, and rather than highs and lows, you experience more of varying levels of contentment." Jack found himself rambling, and wondered if Gabe detected it. He looked at her, and saw she wasn't buying it. He was too curious to let it pass. "You obviously think differently, Richards."

Gabe looked down into her coffee cup, then back at him. "You want to know what I really think, Dr. Stegall?"

"Sure."

"I think you did a fantastic job, and if you don't feel great about it, maybe it's because you're upset by the whole defective implant thing."

"That's an interesting opinion. Why should I be affected by that? I never used the lens."

"I know. But doesn't it make you mad? The lens was never properly tested, and everyone is keeping quiet."

"Mad? No. I mean yes, but not really." Jack was losing his keel. Every so often a medical student would challenge his performance, but in the confrontational manner of a student hung up on impossible ideals and outspoken about patient advocacy. He dismissed their complaints easily. Gabe was different. She was challenging him, but somehow she made him feel—he searched for the word—accepted. And something else. He felt a kindness, a forgivingness, almost a lovingness in her voice. "No, I don't think I'm angry about it," he concluded. "Just careful to protect myself."

"Defensive medicine?"

"I don't know about that," he replied, shifting nervously on his feet. "Anyway, with that implant, the damage has already been done, the water already under the bridge. I'm just doing my job, and making sure I don't get caught in the backwash."

"You—" Gabe stopped, suddenly stood up, and turned for the door. "I better get back with my group."

"Why?"

Gabe stopped, faced him, and took a deep breath. "Well, you say the damage has been done. OK, then, what about FERK? Free Electron Refractive Keratectomy? That's not water under the bridge. It's happening right here and now, and I just think it should, I mean, must affect you to just have to stand by idly and watch it happen. FERK must make you feel so furious."

Jack looked at Gabe with amazement. "What are you talking about?"

Gabe sat down and looked him straight in the eye. "Dr. Stegall, I didn't want to bring it up in the operating room. I thought I might look stupid. But what about the big article on FERK and Metrocare in Time magazine?"

"What article?"

"What artic..!" Gabe didn't finish the word, but instead silently mouthed the word "Oh". She quickly reached into her tote bag and pulled out the magazine.

"Look at this," she said, turning to the page entitled "New York City's Metrocare to be Mecca for Myopia." She handed it to him.

Jack sat down and read. "This is incredible!" He looked up, and beheld Gabe's beautiful, expectant face. "Look, Gabe. I'm going to tell you something in absolute confidence. Two weeks ago my associate Dr.

Giardano told me that the preliminary FERK surgical trial showed serious post-operative corneal scarring."

"In all the patients? Right away?"

"No, it takes time, maybe over a year, for the haze to set in completely. But it showed up in a third of the cases, and Giardano thinks it will reach 50 percent."

"My God!"

"Giardano said that the trial results were so disastrous that he would cancel all FERK operations, notify the Food and Drug Administration, period. He said he was going to announce it at the next committee meeting. And now this. I just do not understand. This is so wierd."

"Weird, or worse."

Jack looked down at the article, and searched in his mind for some half-sane explanation. Finally it came to him. "Publicity," he said, slapping the magazine down on the table top. "It must be that."

Gabe frowned. "But Time magazine has gone on the line saying that Royster really is going to start doing FERK on normal people with myopia. People like you, like me."

Jack removed his paper shoe covers and tossed them in the waste basket. "I can't believe that. I think he and his company know the FERK surgical trial has failed, and he let this Time article run anyway to spread his name around."

"It's so crummy. I just don't see how hospitals and doctors can do stuff like this. I think we should report this to someone."

"Who outside of Dr. Giardano?

"I don't know. There should be somebody."

"You're right. There should be. But there isn't. It's only Dr. Giardano. I promise I'll talk to him right after class."

Chapter *Eight*

11:26 a.m.

Jack led the way down the corridor to a set of double doors marked Surgical Conference Theatre. They entered the semi-darkened theatre complex, and Jack stopped at the door to the right marked Control Room.

"Charlie Finnerty should be here to run my slides," Jack said, patting his briefcase where he kept the Kodachromes. "He's the communications engineer for this place." He thumbed the intercom button at the side of the door. "Charlie, you there? It's Jack."

A voice came back over the intercom. "C'mon in," and the door unlocked with an electronic buzz. Jack and Gabe entered and took the three steps up to the control room, a huge telecommunications cockpit lined with consoles filled to capacity with video, audio, and computer equipment, and fronted by a wide plate glass observation window overlooking the conference theatre itself. Adjacent to the room was the 24 track sound recording studio, complete with its own soundproof recording chamber.

Charlie, a trim man in his 40s, was dressed comfortably in his usual dark maroon sweater, khakis, and sneakers, and happily at work in front of one of the video-computer workstations, his Irish-featured face greenish-yellow in the glow of the monitor. "Be with you in a sec," he said over his shoulder with a tart Boston brogue. "Just finishing up on a video edit. There!" He pressed the "Alt" computer key, and stood up. "Hello, Jack. Hey, you park in the garage like me. Did you hear?"

"The murdered woman? Yeah."

"Hey, you're an eyeman. I was talking to this detective who was snooping around over there. He said the woman had something written down in her pocket about the eyes."

"What did it say?"

"I dunno. Just some word referring to eyes, the guy said."

"Was it a prescription? The woman was very nearsighted."

"No, just some word with 'eyes' in it."

Jack and Gabe exchanged puzzled looks.

Charlie shrugged and switched off two computer monitors. "Anyway, professor, whatcha got for me this morning?"

"Lecture slides." Jack placed them next to the projector. "It's for the 4th year medical student group. This is Gabe Richards, my assigned student. Charlie, give me a sound check on the mike, OK?"

"You bet. Oh, the mike, the mike. Mother of Mary, I completely forgot. I was supposed to tell you. Your lecture. Miss Craig called from the OR. She said you only have a half hour. Absolutely gotta be out of here by noon so that they can get in here for their hookup."

"I don't understand." Jack said. "Noon? Who are they'?"

"I dunno, some heavy-duty televised surgery thing is going on here tomorrow and Thursday. I think they're from Channel 7."

"Televised surgery?" Jack frowned. "Who's the surgeon?"

"Nobody tells me. Anyway, they have a big crew coming over to check out all our gear. Sorry."

Only half an hour, thought Jack. He'd have to slash his lecture in half. There would be little time for questions, and no time to discuss myopia surgery and FERK as he'd promised Gabe. Probably the safest thing anyway, he thought. Best avoid saying a word about FERK until he talked to Giardano. "Half hour it is, Charlie," said Jack. "Get those slides ready. I'm gonna be flying."

Jack and Gabe left the control room and entered the theatre. A hybrid of corporate comfort and high-tech, it was finished in beige and burgundy and looked brand new. Ten curved rows of cushioned chairs faced a stage flanked by two solid mahogany lecterns. At the rear of the stage was a wall of twelve contiguous television monitors. Behind each lectern stood an accessory rack of VCRs and controls. The wall to wall carpeting was of a deep, firm pile, and a slow bass line of soft rock music emanated from somewhere in the room.

Suddenly the lights dimmed, the music faded, and a projection screen silently descended in front of the television monitors. As Jack stepped up to the lectern on stage right to check out the mike, Gabe settled herself in the third row. Moments later the rest of her student group began to drift in and take seats, some in street clothes, some still in their green scrubs, all abuzz with stories of the morning's surgical exploits. Soon all nine medical students were present, except Maria.

"Have you seen Sanchez?" Gabe asked the student sitting directly in front of her.

"No. Probably still stuck in the operating room," came the answer.

"Damn." Gabe fumbled into her tote bag and produced a fresh spiral notebook.

Jack checked the wallclock, and with a flick of a switch the room dimmed further, leaving the lectern illuminated. He introduced himself and began. "I'm here to talk to you about the common optical deficiencies of the eye which require so many of us to wear glasses or contact lenses. Let's start with definitions. How about nearsightedness? And what is the synonym?"

Gabe raised her hand. "Nearsightedness is when, without a corrective spectacle or contact lens, objects beyond a certain distance are out of focus. Of course the synonym is myopia."

"Good. Now, farsightedness?"

A petite, bespectacled Chinese-American student in a pink and white polka dot dress sitting in front of Gabe, raised her hand. "That's when distance vision is better than close."

Jack made out the student's name tag—Anne Chen. "Good, Chen. How about astigmatism?"

A student in the front row spoke up. "There's a curve on the front of the eye."

"Astigmatism is warped vision," said Jack, "when the cornea is shaped more like the surface of a football than a basketball. And presbyopia?"

The students were stumped.

"I'll give you a hint. Nobody here has it yet."

"You're forgetting me, Jack." The voice came over the loudspeakers. It was Charlie, standing behind the observation window in the back, speaking into a control room mike.

Jack smiled. "That's Charlie Finnerty, our communications engineer. He has presbyopia, and the glasses to prove it." As the students turned to look back, Charlie removed his reading glasses and held them up behind the observation window in full view. "How about a definition of presbyopia, Charlie?"

"It's a trick nature plays on you when you get older," Charlie said. "Your arms become too short to read."

"It certainly seems that way," added Jack. "Presbyopia refers to the gradual loss of our ability to focus our eyes on near objects as we age. Now, who here has nearsightedness?"

Four hands shot up, including Gabe's and Anne Chen's.

"Anyone here farsighted?"

A student directly behind Gabe removed his thick glasses and raised them high in the air.

"Leaving one person with glasses unaccounted for," he said to the student in the first row. "You probably have astigmatism."

The student laughed and lifted his glasses away from his face. "Right, pure astigmatism."

After explaining the barest essentials of human optics and refractive errors, Jack pointed to one of the nearsighted male students. "Help us out, and pass your glasses around."

He removed his glasses. "They're pretty dirty," he said with embarrassment as he handed them to Gabe sitting to his left. She held the glasses up to the light and scrutinized the rims.

"As you inspect her glasses," Jack said, "you'll see that they are concave lenses that are thinner in the center and thicker at the rims. Concave lenses bend light rays out."

"They are way too thick at the edge," complained the owner of the spectacles. "Everytime I have my prescription changed, the rims have gotten a little thicker. I'm afraid all the reading in medical school is going to make me completely blind."

Suddenly an image of the murdered woman popped into Jack's mind. Again he wondered what she saw—or could see—at the moment of her death. And why her glasses had disappeared. And how strong her glasses were.

"Anybody here know how strong nearsighted glasses can get?" Jack found himself asking.

The students were stumped.

"As high as 20 diopters," Jack said. "A diopter is the unit of measurement of lens power. If you are nearsighted, the diopters are labeled 'minus,' like 'minus 9 diopters.'"

Looking directly through one of the lenses, Gabe spoke up. "Dr. Stegall, there's something else about nearsighted glasses. Everything looks smaller through the lens." She passed the glasses on to the student to her left. "Why so?"

"Concave lenses always have that minifying effect," Jack answered. "It's one of the reasons why nearsighted glasses are considered uncosmetic. The eyes and the upper face behind the lenses look smaller."

Gabe caught Jack's glance. In the soft lighting she looked more beautiful than ever. He had to make an effort not to stare. "Now, the farsighted student in the fifth row. Pass your glasses around for comparison."

The student complied, then put his hand over his eyes and pretended he was blind, drawing a laugh from the class. When the spectacles reached Gabe, she almost dropped them.

"Watch out, he needs those," Jack said. "He especially needs them to read with."

"I didn't expect them to be so heavy," said Gabe. She held them up to the light. "They're thicker in the middle, unlike the myopic glasses which were thicker at the rims."

"Good observation," said Jack. "Convex lenses are always thicker in the middle."

"Everything is magnified through these lenses," Gabe added. "Just the opposite of the nearsighted glasses."

Jack nodded and looked at his watch. Time was up, and he asked for final questions.

"How about the new operation for nearsightedness, FERK?"

Jack expected the question, but to his surprise, it didn't come from Gabe. It was from the student to her right in the pink and white polka dot dress, Chen, the Chinese-American student.

Jack looked back through the window of the control chamber. There was still no sign of the TV people. He had no choice but to answer.

"OK. Free Electron Refractive Keratectomy. First, remember that nearsightedness occurs when the front corneal window of the eye is too curved or when the eye has overgrown in diameter. We can't surgically shorten the eye, so that leaves the corneal curvature to work with. Almost all the surgery in one way or another makes the curve of the cornea flatter so it bends light rays less. Thus the nearsightedness is reduced. In FERK, you have a million dollar free-electron laser driven by a linear accelerator. The double-barreled laser is positioned over the eyes, and its powerful short ultraviolet radiation is fired at the corneas in bursts. The radiation breaks molecular bonds, literally vaporizes the tissue, and the corneas are flattened. It's done under local anesthesia, but it takes only a few seconds. Clinical trials are fully underway here at Metrocare, under the watchful eye of the FDA. But..."

Jack hesitated. The words wouldn't come out.

The entire class looked at him expectantly.

"But FERK is still an experimental operation."

"Experimental?" asked Chen, looking concerned.

"Yes," said Jack. "And it's very possible that the initial surgical trials which have been started here at Metrocare could..." Jack looked at Gabe, who returned the look with alluring but unflinching eyes, "...run into significant problems with corneal healing."

Damn! Zip your lips, Jack thought, collecting up his note cards. Then the Time article flashed across his mind, and the words just poured out. He looked up, "Remember this. The eye may still grow, and the near-sightedness worsen accordingly, even up into our 40's. Therefore, any procedure to correct nearsightedmess is like trying to give a growing child a pair of shoes which will fit forever."

"My God, then you're even saying that myopia surgery is not only experimental but it may be shooting at a moving target?" It was Anne Chen again, looking excessively worried.

"Yes." Me and my big mouth, Jack thought.

Chen abruptly closed her notebook and shot up from her seat. "Please excuse me, Dr. Stegall." Pencils and paper spilling, she stumbled from the aisle and rushed to the back of the theatre, extracting a cellular telephone from her purse before disappearing through the door. Puzzled over the peculiar departure, Jack glanced at Gabe, who looked just as perplexed as he.

Charlie's voice was heard. "Jack, I just got a call from downstairs. The TV guys want to get in here right away."

Jack dismissed the class, and all of the medical students left the theatre except Gabe, who walked up to the lectern.

"What in the world is with Chen tearing out of here?" Jack asked, noticing how Gabe's lips and eyes caught the light. Stay professional, he coached himself. Personal feelings didn't belong.

Gabe looked around at the now empty seats. "Beats me. I only wish my roommate Maria had been here. I know it sounds silly, but she is so psyched up about FERK. I just don't know why she missed it."

"She's the one assigned to Dr. Royster?"

"Correct."

"My guess is he convinced her that staying in the OR with him was more important. Let's take a look."

Gabe blinked uncomprehendingly. "How do you mean?"

"With MegaMOM, the system. You only saw part of it's capabilities in the operating room. Here, I'll demonstrate it."

Programming through the audiovisual controls and computer keyboard built into the lectern, he brought the stage's entire panel of video monitors to life. "See?" he said. "A video display of each of the 15 operating rooms."

Each monitor was selecting the panoramic camera view of its respective room. Some monitors added a window in an upper corner to show another camera angle, closeup, or microscopic view. Except for two rooms which were totally vacant, and one which showed an orderly mopping the floor, all of the operating rooms were in the middle of surgery.

"I think Royster is Suite 13. Yes, there he is." Jack pointed to the top left monitor. "Looks like he must be on his second case. Let's see if we can find our missing Maria."

Jack manipulated a lever on one of the panels, and the view began to slowly shift. "Not there. Let's pan the robotic camera to the other side."

The view slowly shifted to Royster's right, until the masked face of Maria appeared, looking over an assistant's shoulder into the operative field.

"Fantastic," Gabe said. "You can look at any operation, at any angle, remotely from here."

"More than that," Jack explained. "You can send the audiovisual signal from any operating room to any monitor or set of monitors in the OR or for that matter in the hospital. The system has total flexibility. And you can audiovisually communicate with any room. In fact, there's Cissy now preparing room 14, the room we were working in." He flicked a switch. "Cissy, can we talk to you by the pancam?" The lectern mike picked up his voice.

"Is that you, Dr. Stegall?" came Cissy's voice over the audio, with a trace of echo from the empty operating room. Jack and Gabe watched her as she walked up to the camera.

Jack flicked another switch, and a closeup of Cissy's face filled the monitor.

"I'm showing Gabe MegaMom from the Surgical Conference Theater. Show us the replay capability from there, would you? Cue up my case this morning."

Cissy went over to the AV rack, keyed in the patient's name and the date, and a few seconds later a video replay of Jack's corneal transplant appeared in the upper right hand corner of the monitor.

"Look," said Gabe. "There's the scarred cornea, just before you removed it."

"And I can control the tape from here," Jack said.

"Can you fast forward?" asked Gabe.

Jack moved to a different console, hit a series of keys, and the tape blurred into forward motion.

When regular play resumed, Cissy's voice was the first to be heard, "If de cornea get hazy, de vision go crazy."

Jack hit rewind. This time it was his own voice. "This was the woman who was murdered in the garage…"

"You there, Dr. Stegall?" It was Cissy's live voice.

"Still here," Jack said. "I'll see you tomorrow when I do my pediatric eye case. When do I start?"

Cissy keyed in on her computer, and the schedule appeared. "You're starting second, after Dr. Goldstein's glaucoma procedure. Dr. Royster follows you."

"Royster? What's he doing?" Jack asked. "Royster's surgery days are always Monday and Thursday."

"That's funny," said Cissy. "It's left blank, but he has the eye room reserved for three hours."

"Three hours? Why?"

"I guess Miss MegaMoM made a computer error," offered Gabe.

"Maybe you're right," said Jack. "Thanks, Cissy." He hit a switch, and the image returned to the wide angle view of the suite.

"Unbelievable system," said Gabe. "Where is it run from?"

"The master controls are at the nurses' station. Most of it's already programmed. That way the computer already knows not to telecast rectal polyps to the cafeteria."

"Who controls the computer?"

"Miss Craig, except for override. Dr. Bankert sneaked it into the program," replied Jack, gathering up his notes. "Any operating room can override the central controls for short periods of time. Leaves us a little autonomy." Jack looked over at the screen showing Suite 10. "There's Dr. Matthews beating somebody's brains out. Look. He's on his third case already."

"Is that unusual?" asked Gabe, tucking her notebook into her shoulder bag.

"Not for him. He operates very fast. Fast Fred."

"That's what they called the guy who pierced ears in high school, Fast Frank or something. And this Dr. Matthews is a brain surgeon?"

"Yep."

"Fast unnecessary surgery?"

"No comment."

Gabe cringed. "Not on my brain."

Jack touched the "Escape" key to turn off the monitors. "Time to talk to Giardano. Ready?"

"Where you go, I go."

CHAPTER *Nine*

12:38 p.m.

"I'm sorry, Dr. Stegall. The computer sign-in log says Dr. Giardano isn't here." The Ophthalmology Department receptionist, a thin, young woman with short red hair, tapped the computer keys again. "No, I don't think he's come in."

Jack, standing with Gabe at the reception window, leaned over the counter to view the screen himself. His partner's slot on the screen was indeed blank.

"He probably forgot to punch in," Jack said. "Thanks."

He turned and saw Gabe admiring the general reception area, tastefully furnished and decorated in taupes and grays. Already a few patients had arrived for their afternoon appointments.

"Pretty well laid out, don't you think?" said Jack. "The reception desk is centralized and gives a complete view of the patients coming and going." He couldn't resist the urge to impress Gabe with the layout. "Ophthalmology moved over here a couple of years ago. Occupies the entire western half of the wing."

"Very nice," said Gabe as they proceeded past the reception desk down the corridor to the clinical area of the wing.

"We have 16 private doctors' offices here." Jack gestured towards the doorways and passageways leading off from the corridor. "All of the offices are commonly served by the central reception area, business office, as well as a multi-use eye laser surgery suite, minor surgery rooms, and diagnostic suites. Our office—Dr. Giardano's and mine—is just ahead." He pointed to the door at the end of the corridor.

Seated at the desk facing the door was the secretary, Miss Doris White, an exhausted-looking plain woman in her 50's, conservatively dressed in a dark blue dress and modest pearl choker. Looking up through executive bifocals, she waved at Jack and Gabe as they entered. "Welcome back, Dr. Stegall. We missed you."

Jack returned the greeting, then immediately noticed that her desk was even more submerged in patient charts, bills, and insurance forms than when he had left, the legacy of the computer which, having been installed to battle Medicare and managed care health insurance companies and their blitz of red tape and reimbursement errors, had crashed the month before. Her 3 extra telephones, each blinking on speakerphone, played the recorded message of an insurance company she waited for to come on the line to debate an underpayment or denial. Behind her stood the card table they had set up to hold the unpaid Medicare claims alone. The piles were higher than ever. The countless hours he, his partner, his secretary, and the computer consultant had spent trying to decipher the new three-inch thick manual of cryptography Medicare called its new regulations had failed. Jack shuddered to think how much further the office income had plummeted in his absence.

Seeing Jack survey the reimbursement wreckage, Miss White became teary. Jack knew the toll the job had taken on her. When she had started in the office four years earlier, she was cheerful and optimistic about taking on the work. Since then, the daily beating by third party payors and angry patients had driven her to Prozac. Knowing that the reimbursement debacle would only get worse, and with competent secretaries increasingly hard to find, Jack and his partner lived in constant fear she would burn out completely and quit.

He introduced Gabe, the two women shook hands, and he tossed his briefcase on the couch. "Is Dr. Giardano with a patient?" Jack nodded towards the door to his associate's private consultation office. "I have to talk to him."

"I'm sorry, Dr. Stegall," she answered. "He isn't in."

He took the whole day off to prepare. It's the Dranitzke case." Her lips pursed.

"Which case?" asked Jack.

She glanced doubtfully at Gabe.

"She's OK," Jack said.

Miss White's voice lowered. "You know, Dr. Stegall. The Dranitzke case. That malpractice suit. The patient who went blind after Dr. Giardano's corneal transplant."

"What?" exclaimed Jack. "How is that possible? Last month Dr. Giardano told me his attorney was certain Dranitzke and his lawyer would drop the suit."

"That's what we, I mean, the attorney thought. But they're not dropping it. Dr. Stegall, it's just unbelievable. We think they're suing for…" Suddenly her voice went dry. She grabbed her iced tea, took a long sip, and cleared her throat. "We think they're suing for two million dollars." Her voice was down to a whisper.

"You can't be serious," gasped Jack.

"Yes. Two million. It's sickening. Just sickening."

"My god," said Gabe. "Does malpractice insurance go up to…?"

"That's just it," declared Miss White. "Dr. Giardano is only covered up to a million per case."

"Weathering a suit is devastating enough." Jack shook his head slowly. "But a two million dollar award? It would cut into our corporate assets, maybe even Bob's personal assets."

"It's all so awful," Miss White said. "Anyway, Dr. Giardano is to be interviewed, I mean deposed, by the attorney for the plaintiff tomorrow afternoon, and he took today off to prepare for the ordeal. It's taking a lot out of him, Dr. Stegall."

Jack sensed Miss White's first concern was the same as his: Dr. Giardano's heart condition. "He must be a nervous wreck. Where can I reach him?"

"That's part of the problem," she said. "He was planning to review all of his notes on the case over the weekend, but was on call for the emergency room. He had two eye emergencies back to back. Spent practically the entire weekend in the operating room. Then his car broke down, so he didn't come in today at all, just stayed at home. Said he's absolutely unavailable to everybody until tomorrow morning. I tried to convince him to work here in the office. You know, his wife doesn't get back from her vacation in Italy until Thursday, and I just don't think he should be alone like this. This is all so…"

"You're right," said Jack. "This just isn't like him. Going incommunicado. It's so—extreme."

"He is totally obsessed with the matter. I'm so glad you're back. It will help him so much when he sees you tomorrow. He'll be in around noon."

"When's the deposition?"

"Around 1:30."

"Good. I'll have time to discuss the suit with him beforehand. But I also have to talk to him about Royster's FERK project." From the way Miss White nodded, Jack could tell she was unaware of Royster's Time magazine article.

Jack tilted his head to scan the appointment book perched precariously on a stack of Medicare insurance forms. "Anything here for me this afternoon?"

"I kept your schedule clear…" Her phone rang. "Excuse me Dr. Stegall. This could be the HMO I've been chasing after for weeks."

While Miss White took the call, Jack and Gabe sat down. Jack looked on the endtable with the magazines. The latest Time issue lay there, untouched. Obviously Giardano hadn't gotten to it either.

"Oh, my goodness," Miss White said to her caller. She grabbed a notebook and scribbled rapidly. "No, she isn't a patient. Yes, sir. I will tell him, but he doesn't get back until tomorrrow." She hung up, looking paler than before.

"What is it?" Jack asked.

"Dr. Stegall, that was the police. There was a woman murdered on Friday .."

"Yes, I know. In the garage."

"The police found some things in a pocket. One was a piece of paper with Dr. Giardano's name and an appointment time written down. 8:15 Friday. Oh, dear."

"Dr. Giardano know her?"

"Yes and no. It was very strange. The woman had called Giardano the day before and said she had some information…" Again Miss White looked at Gabe doubtfully.

"It's OK," Jack said. "Go on, please."

"She didn't give her name, but she said she had some new information about that laser operation, you know, Dr. Royster's FERK operation. She was very upset. She said it had something to do with her younger brother. Dr. Giardano was really disappointed when she didn't appear for her meeting with him. Now this. Oh, my goodness. This city is so dangerous."

"What else did they find?" Jack asked.

Miss White handed him the scribbled notes. Jack read them aloud. "A comb, lifesavers, and, what's this, Miss White?" He handed back the paper.

"CLC? That's a contact lens case. They found a plastic case with two lenses. They wanted to know if she was his patient. Of course, she wasn't."

Jack could tell Gabe was reading his mind. "Miss White, please call the police back. Tell them I asked to look at the contact lenses. They can use a police courier. I may be able to give them more information from the lenses."

Miss White wrote down Jack's instruction. "Oh, Dr. Stegall, there was something else." She turned her notes over and read the other side. "The police said that the woman had the word 'lasereyes' written down, too."

"That must be what Charlie was talking about. May I see?" Miss White showed him the word.

"Why did you put a period after the word?"

"I didn't. The police read it to me that way."

Gabe looked at the notes. "Probably a dot. Could be a website. Lasereyes dot something. Dot org, dot com."

Jack handed the notes back to Miss White. "When you call the police tell them this could be a website. They should check it out. Gabe and I will be inside."

Jack led Gabe into his office and sank into the swivel chair that faced his desk, also covered with insurance reimbursement paperwork. Gabe surveyed the room with its armamentarium of computerized ophthalmic instruments.

"Can you believe it, Gabe. Those corneas came from a woman who wanted to talk to my partner."

"Who is being sued, right?"

"Right." Jack sat down and rubbed his temples. "It's the Dranitzke case. Alfred Dranitzke came to Dr. Giardano last year. His left cornea was scarred from a herpes infection and needed a corneal transplant. Before doing it, Dranitzke became a volunteer for Royster's FERK surgery.

"What went wrong?"

Jack got up to fetch his white lab coat from the back of the door and exchange it for his sport jacket. "Dranitzke was one of the very first patients. After the FERK was done, the cornea developed scarred and never healed completely. Dr. Giardano went ahead with the transplant, and did a beautiful job. But after the operation Dranitzke got drunk, fell down, and hit the eye. Remember those stitches you saw me sew in this morning?"

"The ultrafine nylon ones you can't even see with the naked eye?"

"Those. In Dranitzke's eye, the cornea was so weakened and thin, when he fell and struck his eye, they all ripped loose, the graft fell out, and everything in the eye came out with it. The eye was totally blinded."

"Horrible. But why the suit?"

"Something about the sutures Dr. Giardano put in." Jack flopped back in his chair. "The point is that transplant tore out because the patient had the FERK operation to begin with, and then became scarred and weak. The eye went blind because of a FERK surgeon and a drunken patient, not my partner." Jack frowned. The fingernail dug in. "It is so absolutely unbelievable that this suit is being pursued. Especially when a high percentage of these FERK cases turned out to have corneal healing problems, you know, the scarring, the hazing. Drantitzke was just one of many."

"But only Dr. Giardano and Royster know that."

"I have to talk to Giardano. And I want to hear more about this mystery woman who was murderd."

"Do you think those contacts will tell much?"

"Maybe. It may say something about who she was. But I'd like to know what information she had about the laser operation." He looked at the notes Miss White had given him. "And why was she coming to Dr. Giardano?

Jack's belt-pager beeped twice. He looked at the numerical readout, picked up the phone, and called the emergency room. "This is Dr. Stegall," Jack said to the nurse answering. "You have something?"

"Oh, yes," came the voice over the phone. "You're the ophthalmologist on emergency call today. We have a 22-year-old patient here with acute bilateral eye pain. She slept in her hard contact lenses."

"Be right down." He hung up and saw the question on Gabe's face. "Woman with contact lenses problems, Gabe. Fortunately, this one is still alive. God, what is going on around here?"

CHAPTER *Ten*

1:46 p.m.

When Jack and and Gabe reached the central desk of the emergency room, the head nurse immediately put her telephone call on hold. "Oh, good, Dr. Stegall. The senior eye resident is still tied up in the OR with Dr. Royster. This is the chart. Dr. Baker saw the patient."

"Baker's on duty?" Jack looked up from the chart to see if his occasional handball partner was in sight.

Someone tapped his left shoulder. "Hey, eyeballman, how was your vacation?"

Jack turned. It was Dr. Baker, a tall, lean, African American with a gray-flecked crewcut and a white lab coat weighted down with the diagnostic paraphernalia of a city hospital emergency room physician. Not one but two stethoscopes hung around his neck.

"Great, Ed," Jack said. Dr. Baker was a friend, and in the transient, competitive world of medicine, friends were hard to come by. They shook hands, and Jack turned to Gabe. "He and I go back together, what, to the 80's? We were both at Columbia. How's it going?"

"We're getting hit bad." Dr. Baker's easy smile contrasted with dark, serious eyes. "Mercy Park homeless, they're coming in a lot. You hear about the murder?"

Jack nodded as he scanned the emergency room. Even with its 25 bays and four critical suites, the place was a disaster in slow motion.

Patients on stretchers, waiting for X-ray, transportation, or admission, jammed the passageways. Emergency equipment lined the corridors. To his left the waiting room was packed.

Baker signed a chart handed him by one of the nurses. "Jack, I saw that eye patient and prescribed some drops. Then she left when she found out Metrocare wasn't on her insurance plan." A nurse passed him yet another chart of an awaiting patient. "I'll call you to set up a squash game," he said walking away. "They just refinished two of the courts. Aloha."

"Aloha?" asked Gabe.

"Baker's trying to transfer to Maui General before he…"

Jack was interrupted by a loud thump when the double doors facing Mercy Park flew open. Everyone turned and saw two homeless men carrying what appeared to be a worn canvas field stretcher, bearing an old man who lay on his side and cupped his right eye with both hands. A tall, broad-shouldered policeman followed the trio. Squeezing past a portable X-ray machine and a dozen waiting patients, the stretcher bearers went for the nearest gurney stretcher and laid the canvas stretcher on top, poles extending at both ends. The policeman walked over to the nurse.

"They're all from Mercy Park," the cop said routinely with a heavy Queen's accent. "This old codger got into a fight with a couple of your construction workers."

Jack looked at the injured patient, a black man with multicolored tights and a New York City sweat shirt. His clothes were soiled and spattered with fresh blood, his face cut and swollen.

But Jack recognized him as the old man who had crossed the street in front of his car that morning.

Jack stepped to the stretcher, gently eased the old man's hands from the eye, and saw the lids almost completely swollen shut. Blood oozed from between them.

The list of possible blinding complications of the injury sped through Jack's mind: ruptured eyeball, blood clot behind the eye cutting off blood flow to the eye or optic nerve, fracture of the bone around the optic nerve, causing optic nerve swelling and blindness.

"You've got a pretty nasty injury to your eye, sir," said Jack, taking charge. "I'm Dr. Stegall, an eye specialist. Your name?"

"Quimby. Herman Quimby." The voice was thick, the breath reeked.

"We have to admit you for some tests."

"Oh, oh!" It was the nurse, waving her hands in opposition. "We can't take on this patient, Dr. Stegall. We're understaffed already, and we've got to stop taking these no-pay patients. Can't we just check his vital signs and ship him over to Bellevue?"

Jack turned to the nurse. "This man has a severe contusive eye injury. The eye could be in imminent danger of going blind. We have to evaluate him here."

The nurse looked at Jack to see if he really meant it. He did. Looking back at the old man, she summoned an orderly. "OK, let's get him into Acute Room 2," she barked. "And get that dirty stretcher out of here."

One of the two stretcher-bearing homeless men wheeled and glowered at the nurse. He was a tall, muscular, completely bald mulatto, and wore a fringed cowboy shirt streaked with soot and tucked tightly into worn gray trousers. A large tarnished silver belt buckle bore the inscription, "Don't Be Cruel." Beneath his gnarled forehead only one eye glared—the other was covered with a black patch. Jack noticed that the patch had sunk into the socket. No doubt the eyeball was missing.

The nurse turned and marched down the corridor towards the main desk. When the man shifted his monocular gaze upon Gabe, she looked away and stepped closer to Jack. The big man moved to the end of the stretcher and, as the orderly managed the other end, they slid the canvas and poles out from under the bloodied old man.

Examining the patient on the stretcher, Jack turned his attention from the bloodied, swollen eye to the rest of the face and body. As he did, he heard a voice behind him.

"Why didn't you make an arrest and find out why they did it?" the voice demanded of the policeman, "It was malicious assault without provocation. The poor guy wasn't hurting anybody."

Jack turned. The familiar voice belonged to the second stretcher bearer. Standing defiantly in front of the policeman, he was dressed in worn jeans and a black shirt, over which he wore what looked like a frayed white doctor's lab coat. When the man turned to point in the direction of Mercy Park, Jack saw the word "doc" stenciled in fading green letters on the back.

Though his face was weathered and unshaven, the man was surprisingly handsome, with lean, chiseled features, a wide mouth, and shoulder length sandy hair. An odd assortment of pendants—Jack could make out a cross and a small tin compass—hung from a leather thong around his neck.

When Jack looked at his clear, green-blue eyes, the man looked from the unresponsive policeman to Jack. It was then that Jack recognized him.

Peter Kincaid II.

Dr. Peter Kincaid, Jack's medical school classmate. More than that, he and Jack had interned together at what was then Mercy Hospital. They had been friends.

"I thought that was you in Mercy Park this morning, Jack," Peter said. A smile flickered on his otherwise sad and drawn face. He looked twenty pounds lighter.

Jack stood and stared, dumbfounded.

"I should have said hello, but then you looked like you had alot on your mind. How the hell are you, Jack?"

As they shook hands, Jack's mind raced over the shocking rumors he had heard about the fate of Peter Kincaid after they had finished at

Mercy together. Jack had wondered what really happened, where he was. Now, like a ghost from the past, he appeared out of Mercy Park. "Peter, you…" Jack still couldn't find words.

Suddenly the beaten vagrant Quimby coughed and spit blood onto the sheet of the stretcher. Peter spoke up. "I saw it happen. Two hard-hats knocked him on the ground and kicked him in the face, smack in the eye. The workmen putting up that billboard. Someone should find out who put them up to this. First he was clobbered in the ribs with his own stick." Peter picked up the thick wooden cane from the stretcher. "He's an old vaudevillian, chronic alcoholic, diabetes, neuropathy," he finished grimly.

Peter handed the cane to his menacing companion, who was already cradling the folded canvas stretcher in his arms. "It's OK, Bird, it's OK," Peter said, trying to calm him. "Get this stuff back to my tent. Take it easy."

When the big man hesitated the policeman raised his voice and pointed to the exit. "Ok, Bird. You're not needed here. Take a hike."

The one-eyed man spat into an ashtray, hitched up his trousers with one hand and, carrying the stretcher and cane, stomped off and slammed out the double doors.

"So, Jack, you've specialized in ophthalmology," continued Peter Kinkaid, "and now you're here at Metrocare hospital. That's very good." His tone was one of friendliness towards Jack and deep-seated resentment towards the hospital.

"And," boomed the cop, looking directly now at Peter, "you and I are gonna sit right here while the docs do their work."

"Listen, we'll talk later, Peter," said Jack. He and Gabe followed the nurse and orderly wheeling the injured old man into one of the large acute trauma rooms.

Jack and Gabe hung their white coats on wall hooks, then gowned, masked, gloved and splash-glassed themselves in the routine precautions against AIDS transmission, a possibility distinctly higher in the case of a bloodied, homeless patient. While the nurse took the man's blood pressure and pulse, and a second nurse arrived to insert an IV in the patient's arm and draw preliminary blood samples, one of the emergency room resident doctors walked in to do the initial physical exam.

"I'm Dr. Stegall and this is Gabe Richards. We're from ophthalmology," Jack told the resident. "His vitals are stable. You go ahead while we check out this eye."

"Yessir, be my guest," said the resident politely, gowning and gloving up. He glanced at the bloodied eye. "Jesus, don't think I ever saw a peeper like that before."

The resident went to work while Jack and Gabe examined the injury. "Gabe," said Jack, "gently separate the lids a few millimeters, maybe I can get a look at the eyeball itself. I don't think it'll hurt him. The alcohol is still acting like an anesthetic."

Gabe complied.

"How many fingers can you see, Mr. Quimby?" Jack held two fingers in front of the eye while he masked the opposite eye with his hand.

"Two," said Quimby throatily.

"Do you see any difference between the sight in your hurt eye and your other eye?" asked Jack, covering one eye and then the other with his hand.

"Yeah. It's worse."

"Which is worse?"

"My other eye."

"Your other eye? You mean the left one?" Suddenly he remembered— the other eye was the one Quimby had shielded from the sun earlier that morning.

"Yeah, it's the one that had the ..," Quimby clammed up.

Jack flashed his penlight at the suspect eye, and saw a haze of the cornea. It could only mean one thing.

"Quimby, what happened to this eye?"

"Don't remember," mumbled Quimby.

"You don't remember?" asked Jack, trying to conceal his impatience.

"Yeah. And I don't want no more trouble. Don't remember. Ow!" He yanked his bare foot away from the resident who was testing for abnormal pedal reflexes.

"Take it easy, Mr. Quimby, take it easy," Jack said, handing the penlight to Gabe. "Take a look, Gabe. Do you see the hazy cornea?"

"Yes," she said. Then, whispering, "It looks even worse than the patient's eye you operated on this morning."

"Mr. Quimby, please. This left eye. Did you...?"

Quimby turned his head to the right, and spat bloody saliva into the orange plastic bowl placed next to his head.

Jack was getting nowhere. "OK, Mr. Quimby, let's try and see the back of this injured eye." Jack removed the ophthalmoscope from the wall unit and examined the eye's interior. It looked unharmed. When he finished, Gabe released the lids, and Jack spoke to the resident, who was checking the blood pressure. "I guess you know the man was struck in the body with a cane. Ribs, maybe trauma to the abdomen."

"Yeah, looks like someone did a real number on him," the young doctor said. "I've already paged the surgery resident on call to—well, speaking of the devil."

Into the bay strode the general surgery resident, a thick-bodied man with a big jaw and a receding hairline. He was wearing a gray lab coat over his scrub clothes, indicating he'd come down directly from the OR. "All right, what gives?," he asked rudely of the emergency room resident, totally disinterested in Jack's and Gabe's presence in the room.

"Eye trauma, upper abdominal trauma, alcoholic intoxication, diabetes," answered the resident.

"I'll take it from here," muttered the surgery resident.

Jack and Gabe left the bay and walked up to the central desk when a nurse called out. "Dr. Stegall, we just found out. Your patient, the old man. He's got insurance."

"Insurance? Are you kidding?"

"No. He's on Medicare."

"Medicare?"

The nurse shrugged. "Look, it's here on his chart. Medicare of New Jersey."

"New Jersey?" Jack checked the chart. "So it is. That's a first. We'll be able to admit this patient after all."

Gabe looked at the wall clock. "I'm supposed to sign out now up in the OR."

Jack and Gabe agreed to meet the next morning, and Gabe left. Jack made a final entry in the chart when the phone rang and the nurse picked it up. "It's for you, Dr. Stegall."

It was Miss White. "Dr. Stegall, the police just called. They'll courier over that woman's contact lenses tomorrow."

"Great."

"They should be here by noon. Oh, and they wanted me to ask you. Do you know what the initials H C N A might mean?"

"Not a clue. Why?"

"They said the woman had a tiny pin on her lapel. It had those letters on it."

"Means nothing to me."

"Oops, that's the other line, doctor. Could you hold for a moment?"

Jack doodled on a prescription pad with the letters H C N A until the secretary came back on the line.

"Oh, my, Dr. Stegall. That was the police again. You were right. Lasereyes is a website. It's actually 'Lasereyes.com.'"

"Did they access it?"

"Yes, but they found out it's temporarily closed because the man who ran it died last week. My goodness."

"Died? From what?"

"They said he was found drowned in his health club swimming pool. He lived here in Manhattan."

"Did they say it was an accident?"

"I asked them that, and they wouldn't answer. But they said something funny."

"What?"

"They said he was a championship swimmer."

CHAPTER *Eleven*

TUESDAY— 7 a.m.

The telephone call from Miss Craig jarred Jack awake. "Dr. Stegall," came her unapologetic voice at the other end of the line, "your case at 9:00 has been postponed until noon."

"Postponed? How come?" Jack asked groggily, sitting up in the bed to fight off the sleep.

"It's the rehearsal, Dr. Stegall," said the OR supervisor impatiently.

"What rehearsal?"

"For Dr. Royster's televised operation on Thursday. The TV people are here to set up and do the run through."

"I'm coming right down."

At that same moment the caravan of gray stretch limousines turned right off of 9th Avenue into the entrance drive to Metrocare Hospital. A parked ambulance partially obstructed the passageway, requiring the limos to swing wide and cut their wheels hard to the right to execute the turn. One after another, each vehicle's left front wheel barely missed the curb adjacent to Mercy Park and plunged through a huge pothole puddle remaining from the previous night's heavy rains, sending massive arching canopies of muddy water across the sidewalk onto the bodies of two homeless alcoholics sprawled next to the fence, asleep. After the third drenching, one of the vagrants awoke, shaking his fist and cursing the limousines. The liveried chauffeurs ignored him and drove on, as if confident that their passengers had not felt the pothole through the massive suspension systems, nor seen nor heard the splashing and yelling through the heavy locked, soundproofed rearward doors.

The limos pulled up to the entrance of the hospital, and in seconds the chauffeurs were holding open the curbside rear doors for their emerging passengers.

Stepping from the last car were three Japanese men, Dr. Koichi Nakamura and his two translators. After exchanging a few words in Japanese, they walked forward to the middle vehicle, from which two Russian men, Dr. Dmitri Vorov and his assistant appeared. First the Japanese translator bowed deeply, and the Russians attempted to follow suit, bending even lower than Dr. Nakamura, whose bow was almost entirely from the neck, brief and dignified. The group walked to the first car from which, after a pause, two occupants emerged.

First came Miss Helga Gutkopf, the German representative, a buxom woman wearing a brown tweed dress, thick glasses, and ink-black false eyelashes.

At last Dr. Royster appeared, smiling and shaking hands with the other two eye physicians. One of the Japanese translators clicked away with his Minolta, then set off a round of bowing. Miss Gutkopf's bow was more of an awkward curtsy, Royster's a stage bow, slow and confident, head cocked slightly to the left, smiling widely throughout, from the beginning to the end.

The three doctors, standing together exchanging collegial pleasantries, formed a tableau of contrasts. Dr. Nakamura, short wiry, bifocaled, and neatly attired in a dark blue business suit, a formal, serious gentleman in his late 40's. Dr. Vorov—tall and paunchy, dressed in slacks, a polo shirt, and a poorly tailored light sports jacket—coarse by comparison, especially when his loud, boisterous laugh accentuated the heavy lines around his eyes and exposed the two front teeth capped with gold. One feature seemed crude and refined at the same time—his salt and pepper hair cut to perfection with a buzzcut.

Of the three, however, Royster, with his aura of self-confidence and charm, was clearly the central, cohesive character. Every feature of his face—his bushy silver-gray eyebrows beneath a full head of curly prematurely graying hair, alert and penetrating blue eyes, straight nose, and wide, well-dentistried mouth—conveyed the air of authority. His taut, tanned body was impeccably attired in a tailored pinstripe charcoal gray Versace suit, complete with a conservatively striped Celine tie and Japanese mother-of-pearl cufflinks. The solid gold wristwatch was a Phillipe Patek Nautilus. He had a low, resonant voice with a slight twang, the latter complemented by hand-tooled Texan cowboy boots which made him seem taller than his actual 5'9" height.

Mr. Emmet Crantz, the new Metrocare Hospital administrator, had been excitedly watching the arrival from the hospital entrance. As if on cue, he descended the steps to greet the doctors and their assistants. Close on Crantz's heels a frantic hospital photographer snapped pictures as fast as she could without tripping down the stairs. A small group of residents and nurses in starchy hospital whites followed close behind.

"Welcome to Metrocare," bellowed Crantz, wiping perspiration from his face. The hefty, middle-aged man had a florid, pock-marked complexion which seemed forever wet or oily, and always kept a handkerchief close at hand, either in his back pocket or in his silver aluminum brief case. "I trust your ride over from the Plaza Hotel was smooth and enjoyable."

"Good to see you, Emmet," responded Royster for the group. After Miss Gutkopf introduced Crantz and the foreigners, the photographer requested a group picture.

"Wait! I almost forgot the buttons. Can't have the pictures without the buttons," insisted Crantz. He placed his silver briefcase into the outstretched arms of an assistant, and popped it open. Inside, a large ziplock bag was filled with oversized, round, gold-colored lapel buttons. Crantz pulled several out and held them up for the crowd. "We thought the gold looked the best. They're great, don't you think?" he said proudly, reading the button aloud. "METROCARE—FIRST IN VISION."

Crantz and Miss Gutkopf merrily pinned a button on everyone within reach, creating a small stir of compliments and jokes in English, Russian, Japanese, and German. After several group photos, the photographer asked for a shot of Vorov and Nakamura standing together.

"This way for the ceremony," announced Crantz.

The group followed him over to the sidewalk facing the billboard, and looked up with a mixture of expectation and puzzlement. Behind them a handful of arriving hospital orderlies slowed to watch.

Crantz turned and faced the group. "Here at Metrocare we are proud to be part of the pioneering revolution in surgery for myopia. The display before you will become the prototype for our marketing strategy." Crantz fumbled with his glasses and referred to a slip of notepaper. "It symbolizes the great partnership between Metrocare and FERK brought to us by the Globe International Corporation and the wonderful American-Russian-Japanese-German collaboration which made this dream come true. Doctors Vorov and Nakamura, would you please do the honors?" Crantz handed each of them the end of a long golden sash connected to the top of the billboard.

Nakamura goodhumoredly counted to three in Japanese. "Ichi, Ni, San". On "san" both men pulled and the drape fell to the ground. The group uttered a collective "aaahh" before breaking into soft applause. The billboard's picture was now complete, and the doctor in the foreground was none other than Royster, wearing a white doctor's lab coat, holding an ophthalmoscope in one hand, and dangling a pair of spectacles from the other, as if he were about to discard them. To the right of his image was written, "Metrocare—Home of the International Center for Myopia."

"You look great, Royster," laughed Vorov, pointing to Royster's gargantuan face. "After FERK you become great Hollywood movie star."

Royster beamed.

Dr. Nakamura, receiving the translation, shook his head in agreement, then repeated with a thin smile, "Hollywood, Hollywood!"

"Yes, Hollywood!" Miss Gutkopf joined in, clapping her hands.

Royster led the way into the hospital up to the Surgery Conference Theatre Control Room. Inside, Charlie Finnerty was carefully listening to instructions from the director, a trim, curly-headed man in his late thirties wearing chinos, a white cashmere V-necked sweater, and topsiders. Behind them a half dozen television studio engineers and technicians were busy checking their monitors.

"Good morning," smiled the director. "I'm Phil Markowitz. I'll be your director for this shoot today and Thursday. We're just about ready here. The script you gave us is very do-able, and with your—what do you call it, Charlie?

"MegaMOM," answered Charlie, studying the color pattern monitor.

"Yes, with your MegaMOM system, and your great engineer here, Charlie, this is duck soup. With the robotic cameras already in place, all we need is a roving camera in the operating suite, and we're in business."

"Excellent," said Royster."

"It'll go fine, Dr. Royster," Charlie said. "They'll just mix the whole live show on the fly on Thursday from here, and feed it live through the mobile truck over to Good Morning, USA at the studios."

Royster nodded.

"Now, when you get back to the operating suite with your Japanese and Russian colleagues, my crew will give each of you two-way headsets, so I'll be in constant communication with you as I run the whole show from here. Basically, today we're going for a dry run of the FERK operation to familiarize everybody, and we want to get some pre-live footage in the can to supplement the live show, right?"

"Very good," said Royster. He reached into his briefcase and pulled out a 3.5 inch black computer disc. "I brought the data disc we told you about. Do you still think we can run the data on the video the way we planned?"

"Yeah, Charlie and our engineers already figured it out. We just scroll your copy and crawl it across the bottom of the screen."

"Perfect!" Now, if you'll excuse me, I have a full house of anxious reporters waiting out there." As the director and Charlie went to work on the data disc, Royster left the control room and moved swiftly down the aisle to join Crantz onstage.

Stepping up to the lectern, the perspiring administrator held his palms up to hush the packed theatre. "Good morning, we'll get this press briefing started. First, a special welcome to the select group of medicine and science newspaper reporters and photographers here with us today." As he went down the list, reporters stood or gave a wave of acknowledgement. "The New York Times, The Wall Street Journal, Barrons, The Washington Post, and The Los Angeles Times. And from abroad, The Frankfurter Algemeine Zeitung from Germany, Japan's Asahi Shimbum, and The London Times. Thank you all for coming."

Crantz wiped his face with his handerchief and continued. "We have invited all of you today to give you an exclusive preview of our revolutionary eye operation. Without further ado, let me introduce our leader, Metrocare's own Dr. David Royster."

With a broad smile, Royster stepped forward, greeted the audience, and began. "Each of you has been invited here to observe and report a truly historic moment in the history of eye surgery. On Thursday, the day after tomorrow, I will perform the world's first Free Electron Refractive Keratectomy to eliminate myopia. Using a powerful lasing photonizer driven by a linear accelerator, I will precisely sculpt the corneas of my patient, thereby eliminating myopia painlessly in virtually a matter of seconds. The preliminary surgical trials of free electron refractive keratectomy on patients with preexisting corneal scars have been completed, have proven highly successful, and have been cleared by the Food and Drug Administration. On Thursday we perform the procedure on an average myopic patient. We are particularly excited to announce that Thursday's operation will be carried live by Good Morning, USA. The entire country and, via satellite, viewers around the world, will be able to witness this event. Let me introduce our director, Phil Markowitz, in the control room. Phil, take a bow."

The audience turned to see Markowitz rise to his feet behind the observation window and clasp his hands in the air in the fashion of a maestro receiving an ovation.

"Today," continued Royster, "you'll be given written background materials about the machine and the procedure, and you'll get to see a dress rehearsal of us televising the operation. On Thursday, we look forward to your returning for the actual live show."

A Wall Street Journal reporter in the back row stood and started to call out a question. An usher walked over and placed a cordless microphone in his hands. "Dr. Royster, with only a pre-market clearance from the FDA, isn't this televised live operation nationwide somewhat premature?"

Royster laughed. "Not at all. Extensive research has already been done on research animals, and our results with the human volunteers is just as successful." He looked at the wall clock. "We're out of time. I'll leave you all in the capable hands of my associate Miss Gutkopf, who represents the coalition of German investors who have helped to make Globe International a reality."

Royster gathered up Drs. Nakamura and Vorov with their interpreters and led the way to the male surgeons' locker room where, after changing into their surgical scrubs, they marched to operating Suite 13. Outside the suite's double doors, they were engulfed by a television crew standing at the ready with three roving cameras, audio, and accessory lighting.

The audio technicians equipped them with wireless two-way headsets, and seconds later the earphones came to life with the sonorous voice of the director from the control room. "OK, doctors, you're all on camera now, and we've got you all looking good, real good, on our monitors here, and you can hear me just as I can hear you. Beautiful, beautiful. The first thing we are going to do is the shot of what will appear to happen last on Thursday, that is, a three shot of you posing after the procedure. In TV land, sometimes we do last things first. A stage manager will help you take your positions in front of Camera 1 in front of the scrub sink."

The stage manager stepped forward to compose the shot. "That's just perfect," said the director. OK, gentleman, next we want to shoot you rolling in the FERK machine from the corridor into the operating suite itself and into position. As you roll it in, our narrator will read—hold it—Charlie, is the narrator ready to go?"

Charlie, sitting at the opposite end of the control room, stood up to look back into the sound recording studio. In the soundproof booth a small elderly man with streaked back silver hair had just put on his head set and was reviewing the script. "All set back there," Charlie replied.

"Good," said the director. "OK. The narrator delivers the material you gave us, Dr. Royster, and we'll give that a try right over the music, and see how it goes."

Royster gave a signal, and four orderlies walked over to a large block-shaped structure draped with a glistening white nylon cover and standing in a side alcove. Leaning their weight into the heavy structure, they rolled it slowly forward to where Royster was positioned. He and Nakamura removed the drape, and for a hushed moment everyone stood and stared.

Over 6 feet tall and almost as wide, the laser photonizer appeared as a gigantic cuboidal robot. On one side was a huge panel with 6 digital displays, 4 video screens, and 3 subpanels of built-in computer keyboards. The treatment arm for the apparatus was a multi-jointed structure with a gray metallic sphere at its tip. At the base of the sphere projected two firing barrels. A set of viewing binoculars was connected to the sphere. Finished in beige bakelite and chrome, the device was suspended on wide-bodied air-inflated tires.

The director continued. "Doctors, if you will each take a position at the rear of the machine, and when I give you the cue, you can slowly roll it into the operating suite and into position in the center over where the operating table will be located."

Dr. Royster broke in. "Instead of a conventional operating room table, we're going to introduce our brand new patient transporter unit with its own attached operating platform. You'll see us set it up in a minute."

The orderlies opened wide both doors to the operating suite. Standing inside were two nurses, gowned, gloved and masked and waiting dutifully for the entry of the machine. "Stage manager," intoned the director, "could you reposition the nurses a little further back? There, that'll be better."

Above, in the observation chamber, one medical student sat and watched, fascinated: Maria Sanchez.

CHAPTER *Twelve*

Unnoticed, Jack entered the conference theatre and took a seat in the back row. Just then the director gave a cue, the music faded, and the baritone stage voice of the narrator boomed: heard.

"Time: today, live. Location: Metrocare Hospital, New York City. For the first time in history, the revolutionary treatment for nearsightedness, Free Electron Refractive Keratectomy, is about to be performed on a normal nearsighted patient. Shown here are the pioneers of the procedure, America's Dr. David Royster, Japan's Dr. Koichi Nakamura, and Russia's Dmitri Vorov, rolling the one million dollar linear accelerator-driven laser into the operating suite." Finally the machine was brought to rest with its firing sphere directly in the center of the room.

"Cut," said the director, "Good. Great. I think we got it fine on one take. Dr. Royster, do you want to bring in the patient transporter now?"

"Absolutely." Royster gave a signal through the open doors to four waiting technicians, who then turned to another large draped apparatus in an opposite alcove. They rolled it up and into the entrance to the suite and undraped it, revealing an enormous, gleaming, stainless-steel, tractor-conveyor device. On the corridor end of the main conveyor belt was a seat containing a plastic manikin clothed in white hospital pajamas. On the opposite end of the apparatus, now positioned directly beneath the firing arm of the FERK machine, was the second seat which had folded out to act as a suspended operating room table.

"That's fine," said Royster. "Now lock the wheels and we're ready to begin." Royster patted one of the rubberized tractor belts. "You will all see that this works somewhat like a Ferris Wheel, transporting each new patient—obviously a manikin for this morning's dry run—from the corridor into the suite and into position for the procedure. The efficiency is unparalleled."

"Beautiful, beautiful!" said the director. "Got a name for it?"

"The Myogoround," Royster replied.

The director held his index finger in the air. "All right. When I say 'action,' you'll get the cue from the stage manager, and then we begin the countdown, the music, and the machinery. Standby everybody. All right—action!"

At the stage manager's cue, Royster touched a switch and the Myogoround conveyor belt began its slow rotation. Simultaneously, a computer voice from the FERK machine began the countdown synchronistically with the red digital display on the timer. "120 seconds, 119, 118…,"

An internal vacuum sucked the mannikin's head back into the head rest as the seat jerked and began to move the dummy upwards into the operating room suite.

"…105, 104, 103…,"

The seatback began to lower, until finally the manikin was in the supine position, descending towards its final position under the FERK machine. When the entire mechanical motion was finished, the head of the manikin was directly beneath the firing sphere, and the empty seat had reached the corridor, obviously awaiting its next "patient" cargo.

The narration continued, "…automatically placing the patient into position for the treatment. Now you see the FERK machine itself, the device which holds the key to eliminating myopia in millions of people worldwide."

"Cut," barked the director. "OK, sterile garments everybody. We'll pick up the action where the countdown left off. Again, when you get your cue. Ready—action!"

The computer voice countdown continued, "…94, 93, 92…," and the narrator went on, "…and now the patient can be seen in perfect position to receive the beam of photonized laser energy."

Royster positioned the FERK firing sphere directly over the manikin's face. The enlarged view of the dummy's fake plastic eyes immediately appeared on the video monitors. One of the nurses placed a drape around the eyes. Royster grasped the placement handles and positioned the aiming beams over the eyes. The music faded up, the lyrical movement from the Mozart Clarinet Concerto.

The director cut in softly. "OK. Are you gentlemen on schedule to fire?"

"All set," said Royster.

At 30 seconds, the narrator came on again. "Preliminary trials on volunteer humans with pre-existing corneal scars have been successfully completed, with excellent postoperative healing." At that moment data began to appear at the bottom of the video, streaming slowly across ticker-tape-style. Switching from his script to the screen, the narrator began to read the stream of data aloud, "Trial patient #1: perfect, clear corneas, no haze, 20/20 vision. Trial patient #2: excellent, corneas clear, no haze, 20/20 vision. #3: excellent, corneas clear, no haze, 20/20 vision. #4: excellent healing, no haze, 20/20 vision. #5: excellent, corneas clear, no haze, 20/20 vision." After the 10th case, the narration shifted back to the written script. "These impressive surgical results have cleared the way for FERK to be offered to the nearsighted here in the United States, and eventually to myopes worldwide."

Jack froze. The displayed data didn't show a trace of the disastrous results Dr. Giardano had told him about. He bounded from his chair and rushed to the wall phone to call Giardano at the Whittaker office.

The line was busy. He tried again. Busy. He returned to his chair and continued to watch, stupified.

It was now Royster's cue. "Let's listen to the countdown. At 15 we'll go to full laser power, at 10 we'll go to ready to fire, and at five I will prepare to fire."

At 20 seconds, Royster tightened his grip on the firing handles. At l5, as Nakamura switched to full power, the machine's hum elevated to a higher pitch. At ten, Vorov locked on to "ready to fire," and at five Royster opened the dummy's plastic lids and leaned forward as if ready to fire.

"Five…"
"Four…"
"Three…"
"Two…"
"One…"

At zero, Royster depressed the foot pedal. Instead of firing, a light illuminated above his scope, "Safety On—No Fire."

"That does it," said Royster.

Chapter *Thirteen*

Jack rushed from the theatre to the dictation room and called his office. He paced back and forth until Miss White finally picked up.

"I'm sorry," she said. "Dr. Giardano hasn't come in yet. But he certainly should be here before noon."

"Have the contacts of the murdered woman been delivered?"

"Yes, doctor. They're right here in my drawer."

"Does the plastic case say anything?"

"No, just a simple pink carrying case with two soft contacts inside."

"I'll be down there right after my case."

He went to the surgeons' locker room to change, and, stepping through the door, stopped short. There, saying goodbye to several reporters while changing back into street clothes, stood Royster. The reporters left, and as Royster pulled on his cowboy boots, he looked up and noticed Jack.

"Hello, Stegall, where you been keeping yourself?" he said, looking back at his boots to inspect the shine.

"Just got back from vacation," answered Jack, hating every syllable escaping his mouth. The first doctor he wanted to talk to at that moment was Giardano. The last, Royster.

"Vacation, huh," Royster said, buttoning the last button of his monogrammed dress shirt. "Caribbean?"

"No."

"I was just down in the Cayman Islands," said Royster, pulling on his pants and adjusting the silk suspenders. "Just bought one of the new 2 million dollar condos right on Seven Mile Beach. New project they call the Grand House. Fantastic spread, fantastic ocean views." He grabbed his toilet kit and walked over to a sink to shave. "Ever been to the Cayman Islands, Stegall?"

"No."

"Some place. Big offshore banking deal there. They have unnumbered bank accounts that are so secret, even the banks don't know they exist." Royster laughed heartily at his own joke.

Jack ignored the vacation one-up-man-ship, and hurried out of his shirt and pants. Then Royster made the remark.

"Those islands are great. Be a good place for someone like you to relocate your practice. Tons of surgery. You'd make a bundle."

The words "relocate your practice," the same that had been used when he was fired in Washington, cut like a scalpel. Seconds later, Jack found himself standing barefoot in shorts and undershirt in the lavoratory, staring at Royster's back. "I saw the rehearsal for the live FERK operation," Jack said flatly.

"Huh?" uttered Royster as if the entire matter was beyond Jack's ken.

"I said, I saw the rehearsal for the live operation," Jack repeated. The fingernail dug in.

"Hey, good, good," said Royster, surprised at Jack's close proximity. "Did you see the Myogoround? Something, huh?"

"Yeah."

Royster began to lather his face. "It's going to be a great show. We'll have a packed house. Media, hospital Board of Trustees. Just found out the Chief of the Eye Department at Columbia, Dr. Koskey, is coming down to watch. I'd like to get that residency affiliation with Columbia."

Nothing new, Jack thought, Royster's equating himself with the Metrocare Eye Department.

Royster rinsed his razor and began to shave. "Great show. Great show. See the video takes, Stegall?"

"The video looked great. But you and I both know that the procedure isn't great."

Royster stopped, and without removing the blade from his lathered face, rotated his head a quarter of a turn and looked at Jack silently. He then turned back to the mirror, and continued the razor's motion. Jack stood, motionless, perplexed, feeling like a man who had swung a wild punch in total darkness at his adversary and was waiting for some retaliatory blow.

Royster looked up and smiled at Jack in the mirror. "Dr. Stegall, you know, I wish you'd been able to come to Japan with me for the last seminar on FERK. We could have brought you up to date."

"That's not what Bob Giardano says."

Royster stopped, this time laying down his razor and turning to face Jack squarely. He seemed to scrutinize Jack, like a boxer taking his measure of a new opponent who had just entered the ring. Jack stared back, mute. Royster toweled his face, went over to the stall. "And just what does Bob say, Stegall?"

"He says that your first human clinical trials showed a high rate of corneal scarring."

For a long moment there was only the sound of urine streaming on the white porcelain.

"Now that is very interesting, very interesting," Royster finally said, facing the tiled wall, "especially coming from someone who does not have official access to the study. But never mind that for right now. When did you last talk to Bob?"

"Two weeks ago. What difference does that make?"

Royster flushed, turned, and zipped up his fly. "All the difference in the world, Stegall." he said, suddenly smiling with confidence. "Giardano and I reassessed the data last week." Royster snatched up his toilet kit, returned to his locker, and swung on his suit jacket. Jack followed close behind.

"Reassessed the data?"

Royster glanced at his $35,000 Patek Phillipe. "I gotta go, those reporters keep you on the run. Ask Giardano about the data. He'll bring you up to date."

"I plan to."

Royster's voice hardened. "Listen, doctor, do you want to know what I think about your—point of view? I think—I think you must be tired, and need another vacation." He laughed with self-amusement. Then, glaring at Jack, his voice became edged. "Stegall, Giardano and I are running the research on this, and, frankly, doctor, you know it's none of your damned business."

"Maybe you've forgotten, Royster. I am an alternate on the research oversight committee."

Royster's eyebrows raised. "But, you're an alternate, and nothing more. So if you don't mind, you are standing in the way." Royster nodded to the narrow passage to the door, and Jack realized he was standing in Royster's path. Jack took a step aside. Royster walked past him, but at the last moment stopped to adjust his Celine tie in the mirror just before the door.

"Dr. Stegall—Jack—arguing is silly," Royster said. The wide smile had returned. "You know, Jack, every new pioneering discovery has always had its detractors. And I think criticism is basically healthy. But you don't know what is really going on with FERK, so let me clue you in. This procedure is going to take off. A revolutionary, world-wide, billion dollar industry. You just have no idea. Who knows, there may be a place for you on our team. When distribution of the machine really picks up, we're going to be looking for people like you to spread the word, the technology."

Royster leaned closer and lowered his voice. "And that means all kinds of ground floor opportunities with Globe, Jack. Preferred stock options." He gave Jack a double pat on the shoulder and disappeared out the door.

CHAPTER *Fourteen*

12:52 p.m.

Fifteen minutes later Jack tapped on Dr. Giardano's private office door, got no response, and walked in.

His partner sat hunched over a cluttered desk, engrossed in copious pages of notes spread before him. On one side of the desk stood stacks of ophthalmology textbooks, on the other a mug of black coffee and the cold remains of a pepperoni pizza. A quick glance at the office revealed that the extensive array of eye examination equipment had been pushed to one side to allow for the placement of three additional chairs facing Giardano's chair, obviously in preparation for the deposition.

"The damned Dranitzke case, right, Bob?" said Jack softly.

Giardano looked up and managed to smile from a face set with anguish. "Jack. How are you?" he said, gesturing for him to sit down. "Welcome back. Jesus. It's good to see you again. Yeah, the Dranitzke case. Can you believe it? Can you believe these people didn't give up suing me for this thing?"

Jack surveyed Giardano's physical condition. He looked terrible. Behind thick bifocals, the heavy bags beneath his eyes were darker than ever. The flesh of his soft, fine-featured face was sagging and lined with fatigue. From the crumpled appearance of his gray suit, Jack surmised that he'd been up all night reviewing the case. Giardano repeatedly swept flat the few remaining strands of gray hair across his half-bald head, a mannerism Jack recognized as a sure sign that the older man was under severe stress.

"Bob," Jack said, "I came in to talk about something, but you look exhausted. Are you sure this is the right time to go through a deposition? How do you feel?"

"Like shit. It's the angina acting up again. I've been popping the nitro tablets like peanuts." Giardano removed a small vial from his coat pocket, snapped off the cap, and slipped a small white pill into his mouth.

"It's outrageous, this suit," said Jack. "What you told me is so obvious. The graft didn't heal well because the previous FERK procedure had weakened the cornea. Dranitzke is a self-neglecting alcoholic to boot. Bob, I'm sure you have nothing to worry about."

Giardano's agonized expression remained unaltered. "I know. And Royster's going to back me up all the way, so I know I shouldn't worry. But it doesn't work that way. I mean, to be sued. Jack, this is the first time for me. I can't seem…"

He stopped talking the instant Miss White tapped on the door. She timidly entered, handed Giardano several more sets of files, then withdrew.

"I can't seem to contain this thing in my mind," Dr. Giardano continued, half-whispering. "To be attacked by a patient, someone you were trying to help. You know you're in the right, but then you start what if-ing yourself, wondering. You start feeling guilty—then you come to your senses and get angry—then guilty because you're angry—I can't explain it—it just does something to you."

"Bob, listen," Jack said quietly, wondering if he was getting through at all. "This Dranitzke is just a crazy man who had a complication from an experimental procedure he volunteered for. When they get the facts straight, they'll drop it. You have got to believe that. Bob? Do you hear what I'm saying?"

Giardano broke from his daze. "God, I hope you're right, Jack."

"This suit isn't going anywhere. Any plaintiff's attorney—who is the attorney, anyway?"

Giardano tremulously sipped on his coffee. "A man named Ed Schurf."

"Schurf?"

"You know him?"

"Yeah. He cross-examined me when I had to testify in a malpractice case a few years ago. Schurf is your typical…," Jack hesitated, "…lawyer." Jack was about to say "snake," but caught himself, realizing he didn't want to upset Bob any further. Jack knew Schurf to be in fact an arrogant bastard, a junkyard dog of a lawyer. But he wanted to give Giardano as much encouragement as possible. "Don't worry about Schurf, he's a turkey, a big, fat one at that. He'll be very obnoxious, very threatening, but just sit back and let your attorney do all the talking. It should go very fast."

"Yeah, my attorney, if he ever gets here. Miss White just told me he's stuck in crosstown traffic. I wish he'd get here. I want to get this damn thing over with."

Miss White knocked on the door and hesitantly looked in. "Dr. Giardano, it's your wife calling long distance from Rome. Will you take the call? She's worried—she got the answering machine from your home all yesterday."

Giardano nodded. "I'll take it, but for Christsake call the building engineer to come down and do something about the ventilation in here, will you? It's way too hot."

"Yes, doctor."

Giardano picked up the phone. "Bon giorno, honey," he said, making an attempt to be cheerful. He listened quietly, again stroking his left hand nervously across his scalp, occasionally interjecting "I know honey, I know," into the conversation. Finally he said, "OK, honey, I'll let Tiny talk to the plaintiff's lawyer, but that's all. No, no direct involvement…don't worry…I promise…Jack is right here…love you...safe flight back." After he'd hung up, he stared blankly at the receiver.

"Everything OK?" Jack asked.

"Oh, sure, sure," said Bob unconvincingly. "She's just worried about me, the deposition, you know. She thinks I should let her attorney brother, Tiny, help out, but I want to keep the rest of the family out of it."

Jack was distracted by the other man's complexion, which appeared even grayer than when the conversation began. "Bob, look, maybe it can wait," cautioned Jack. "I mean, your deposition and everything."

"Hell. I guess I'm as ready for the damned deposition as I'll ever be, staying up all night for all this shit. I have a few minutes now. Miss White told me you've been chafing to see me since you got back from vacation. God, is it about that murdered woman who was supposed to see me? Miss White said you had her contacts sent over here."

Jack took a deep breath. "Well, yeah, it's about the woman, but really it's about FERK. Do you realize what's going on, what Royster is doing?"

There was no misinterpreting the look of guilt that played over Giardano's face. "Jack, I've been meaning to talk to you about it, but you went away, and then I was tied up with..."

Jack cut him off. "Meaning to talk to me? Bob, I don't understand. What's to talk about? You told me only a few weeks ago that the FERK surgical trial data was a flop, plain and simple." Jack spoke as calmly as he could, trying to conceal the exasperation.

"Well, it's actually sort of complicated, Jack, but Royster and I—we—Royster and I re-conferenced on that data, Jack. He—really we—decided that most of the data held up after all, I mean, for the time being."

"The data held up? For the time being? Bob!" Jack retorted. "You told me that almost 50% of the cases had developed corneal scarring!"

"That's true," conceded Giardano. His tone had become sheepish.

"How could any reanalysis of such data justify operating on normal eyes?"

Dr. Giardano set aside the file he was holding and looked up with a deep frown. "Normal eyes? What? What the hell are you talking about, Jack?"

"You mean you don't—Jesus Christ, Bob. Royster didn't even tell you."

"What, Jack? Royster didn't tell me what?"

"Bob! Royster's going to do the new procedure on normal near-sighted people. He's going to perform FERK on both eyes of a normal myope day after tomorrow, and he and the hospital are even going to have it televised live, nationally."

"I don't believe this."

"It's true. They did a dry run of it up in the operating room this morning. Major newspapers are going to cover the show. Royster's been planning it for weeks, maybe months. He got Time Magazine to run a big warmup article on FERK last weekend. And now look! Here's the schedule for the show." Jack unfolded the sheet from his pocket. "See? The TV people and Royster are calling it 'The Myopia Miracle.' They're even planning to display the FERK surgical trial data. Over 25 cases, but every case, every single case, is perfect."

"That son of a bitch!" He slammed his palm on the desk. "I cannot believe this! That damned son of a bitch!" He began to breathe heavily and rock in his chair, as if to find some bodily biorhythm to offset the pain of the rancor assaulting him within.

"Bob, take it easy. What is it? What is Royster doing?"

Giardano grabbed a vial of pills from the corner of his desk and washed several down his throat with coffee. Visibly tremulous, he stood up, went to the slightly ajar door to close it securely, and then turned to face Jack.

"What is Royster doing?" scowled Bob. "I'll tell you what he's doing. He's—he's betraying me, the eye department, shit, betraying the whole goddamn public! The sleazy bastard."

"Betraying?"

"Exactly. Listen, Jack. Oh my God. A few weeks ago, just after I told you, I told Royster about the lousy surgical trial results. He seemed to accept the fact that FERK would have to go back to the drawing boards. But then, a few days later, he came back to me. With a suggestion. He told me that the Russians, you know, the big Russian superstar ophthalmologist?"

"Dmitri Vorov."

"Vorov, yeah. He told me that Vorov had learned to prevent the corneal scarring by using a special eye drop after the operation for a few weeks. Then Royster made this big point that if he didn't get the trial data approved by the Food and Drug Administration, it would set FERK back months, even years, and the competition, the other laser companies, would jump way ahead. And that would be just about the end for FERK, and bad for the eye department and Metrocare. So Royster—Christ, Jack, this isn't easy."

"I understand. Please, go ahead. I'm with you."

"So Royster asked me to—oh, Christ!"

"What, Bob? Royster asked you to do what?"

"He asked me to separate the bad data from the good, and send the good data—it's those 25 cases you saw— to the Food and Drug Administration with the understanding—Jack, he gave me his word, he gave me his goddamned word—with the understanding that while the FDA was giving the good data its approval, Royster would run another series of FERK procedures on corneal scars and prove, I mean, prove to me, that these new Russian drops prevented the scarring. The goddamned bastard gave me his word. Oh, God!" He removed his glasses and buried his face in his hands.

"Please, Bob, try to relax. Look, what's the drop, the medication he was talking about?"

Dr. Giardano slumped back in his chair. "A mixture of zinc sulfate and Vitamin A. But Royster was just using me. Now that he's got his FDA approval, he's rushing ahead to be the first to laser a normal myope with FERK. The bastard lied to me to jump the gun!"

Jack's eyes widened. "Bob, the last thing I want to do right now is upset you further, but I've got to tell you this. The Russians have only used that zinc sulfate-Vitamin A preparation on rabbits. Their study was small, and the results were, well, you know, looked Russian."

"Looked Russian? How do you mean?"

"Russian, you know. One-hundred percent success rates, stuff like that. Bullshit Russian scientific results. So it's very doubtful that those drops work in rabbits, and I'm afraid there just isn't one molecule of evidence that they work in humans."

Giardano stared at Jack quietly, his eyes narrowing.

"Royster's no fool. My God, now I don't even believe that he believes in those drops. Do you?"

Jack shrugged.

"So the drops are just a bunch of—hell, eyewash," Giardano growled. "And he knows it!"

"Let's put it this way, Bob. I don't know what he knows or believes or hopes about those drops, but what he does believe in is being the first person in the world to cure myopia successfully with a laser, and to become very famous and very rich in the process, especially very rich. Everybody and everything comes second to that objective."

A look of confusion contorted Giardano's face. "I don't get it. Famous? Rich? He knows that FERK causes scarring. He'll start out rich and end up sued to kingdom come. What is he thinking?"

"Bob. I just ran into Royster in the OR. I think..."

"What did he say?"

"He said something about stocks, preferred stocks. Bob, I have no proof but…"

"But what? What?"

"He could be taking Globe public."

"Public? That's crazy. When the corneas start to scar, his stocks would drop like a ton of bricks!"

"But that would be after the initial offerings, after Royster and his crew made their millions. They'd be crying all the way to the bank."

"But the scarring. The blindness. The suits!"

Jack paused. "Yes, but Bob, you yourself said the scarring takes time to show up. Remember the defective European implants, the horrible complications?"

Giardano sat up straight. "Cover-up. Of course! They'll be able to cover it all up and ride it out. "Well, this is the beginning of the end for our FERK friend, Jack. I'm going to hang him and his superduper FERK procedure out to dry."

It didn't appear that simple to Jack, not at all. "But the data," Jack said, "the data I saw up in the operating room on the video. It doesn't have a shred of the bad results in it. It's perfect."

"Right. And Royster thinks he has nothing to worry about because he thinks the bad data was deleted, erased. I told him I erased it." Without a word, he walked back to Jack until he was standing directly in front of him. For a moment, he closed his eyes, clasped his hands together, and turned his face skywards in a gesture of prayerful gratitude. When he opened his eyes to look at Jack, he had curious look of mischief. "But I didn't, Jack. I didn't erase it. I couldn't. I separated the bad from the good, yes, and Royster printed out the good data for the FDA and…"

"Printed?"

"Right, printed. He only sent them the good data on hard copy. And now, he's using the good data for this outrageous operation on television. But, Jack, I didn't erase the bad." He sat down. "I saved it. It's all on the disc. Jack, it's all still right on the disc."

Dr. Giardano opened the right upper drawer of his desk, removed a single 3.5 inch black computer disc, and held it up like a trophy.

"That's it? That's the data?" asked Jack.

"Yes. This is the original, and Royster has the only other copy. So, our famous Dr. Royster thinks the bad data was deleted. It's not. He thinks it is, and that's why he thinks he has me by the balls. He must figure that, with no evidence, I could never go to the hospital or the FDA and expose him. Boy, does he have another think coming. The bad data is right on the disc, and when I'm through, Royster is, ha, as my 6 year old grandson would say, 'dead meat.'" He gently laid the disc in the center of his desk.

"Do you have a back-up copy yourself?"

Giardano nodded. "Yes. Miss White keeps it in the committee file."

Jack frowned. There was still the Dranitzke lawsuit. "What about the malpractice action? Will Royster still support you when you go against him?"

Giardano made a fist in the air. "Royster already gave his deposition last Friday. His testimony is in the bag. He can't go back on it."

"Fantastic!" Jack felt himself grinning; it was as if the sun had finally escaped the clouds that had beset him ever since the call from Miss Craig that morning.

Giardano slowly shook his head. "God, I guess she was right."

"Who?"

"My wife Gina. She's the only one—besides you now—who knows about this lousy situation. She begged me from the start not to get involved with Royster's scheme. She called it data-processing. Funny, but not funny. Today she calls me all the way from Italy to ask me again to break off from Royster. I was blind, Jack. Too worried about bolstering the eye department, too caught up in all this marketing push by the hospital, too..." His lip trembled.

Jack squeezed his partner's shoulder reassuringly. "Bob, don't be hard on yourself. Remember, you needed Royster solidly on your side for the malpractice case. You were partly protecting yourself, the office." Jack hesitated. "And for that matter, me."

"That is a fact, Jack," Giardano said grimly. "A two million dollar verdict against me would exceed my malpractice insurance coverage. The office, our corporation, my assets and—that's right, even yours—everything could be put on the chopping block."

He was interrrupted by a rap at the door. Miss White leaned in, looking more nervous than ever. "Dr. Giardano, Mr. Schurf, the attorney, and the court stenographer called. They're in the building and headed here."

"Wait, Miss White," Jack said. "Bring in those contact lenses."

Miss White fetched the case and placed it on Dr. Giardano's desk. Jack picked them up and explained what he had learned about the murdered woman's eyes in the operating room.

"Jesus," Bob said. "Let's read out the lenses right now."

The men walked to a small lab at the rear of the office and placed the lenses in the soft lense analyzer. Both printouts read "Minus 12."

"She had advanced nearsightedness," Dr. Giardano said. "That may be connected to why she was coming to me with information in the first place."

"What did she say?" Jack asked.

"Only that she knew something very important about the FERK operation. She said something about her brother. I wonder…"

"What?"

"Royster mentioned there was something else that had gone wrong with the procedure. He claimed it was minor, but it gave me an uneasy feeling. Now this woman. I wonder if she knew what Royster was talking about. But why? Who was she?"

"Did you get any idea over the phone?"

"She repeatedly refused to give her name. But I got the idea she was a nurse. And she said something about New Jersey…"

"You heard about the website that was closed down?"

"Yes. Very, very strange."

Jack held one of the lenses on his fingertip.

Giardano cocked his head. "What do you see?"

"Look. On the edge of the lens. It says MV. Bob, these are Myopevue lenses."

"So she wore minus 12 Myopevues. Not too many people wear those."

The intercom buzzed. It was Miss White. "They're here now, doctors."

"OK. I'll be ready in one minute," said Giardano. He dropped the disc into the right pocket of his lab coat. "Jack, hold on to those contacts for dear life. Let me get this goddamned deposition out of the way, and then I'll show you the disc on the computer. Maybe there is more on it than even I knew. After that, I have some very interesting phone calls to make to Metrocare administration."

"Crantz?"

"Yes, wonderful Mr. Crantz, and then the FDA."

Chapter *Fifteen*

1:29 pm

A skinny man in his 30's with orangy hair and a small, gold-stud earring in his right lobe sat ourside Giardano's office. Miss White saw the question on Jack's face.

"Bathroom," she said. "Mr. Schurf said he'll be right back." She hung up the phone.

Exiting the office, Jack looked down the corridor and saw an obese man come out of the men's room, still buckling his belt as he headed in Jack's direction. His gelatinous slabs of fat, bulging and billowing in every direction beneath a canopy-sized three-piece suit, jiggled and swayed with each waddling step. His equally blubbery head, a watermelon with black-framed bifocals and male-pattern baldness, merged indistinguishably into a stubby, triple-chinned neck. He carried a heavy, worn leather brief case under one arm, and was holding a half-eaten Twinkie in the opposite hand.

Ed Schurf spoke first. "Dr. Stegall, I believe."

"Dr. Giardano is my partner," Jack said coldly.

"Yeah, saw it on the letterhead," Schurf said over his shoulder as he waddled on towards the office.

Jack turned and walked out to the main reception desk to check the afternoon schedule of patients.

"Oh, good, Dr. Stegall," said a white-uniformed nurse at the desk, holding the patient list in her hand. "Some of Dr. Royster's patients have already arrived. Goldstein is pitching in, too."

"How many of Royster's patients do you need me to see?"

"If you could see three, you will save the day."

"Fine, but my secretary should be left completely free to assist Dr. Giardano, so I'd prefer not to use my office area. Is there a free exam room?"

The nurse looked at the doctors' schedule on the bulletin board. "It's pretty tight. Tell you what. Just use Dr. Royster's office. His secretary went with him to a meeting at the Plaza Hotel, but she left the office open in case we needed it. That should work fine." The nurse handed him three charts, and he walked halfway back down the common corridor to Royster's office on the right.

Passing the secretary's unoccupied desk, he stepped into Royster's private examination suite. Photos of Royster posing celebrities, politicians, movie stars, sports figures, and media personalities covered the walls. One photo showed Royster shaking hands with the Chairman of FDA. Jack sat at Royster's desk, opened up the first patient's chart, and soon was engrossed in the clinical history.

Dr. Giardano stood to greet the two men Miss White ushered into the office.

"Ed Schurf is my name, counsel for Mr. Dranitzke." The corpulent lawyer glanced around the room. "Dr. Giardano, you told me, am I not correct, that you would have counsel present for this deposition?"

"I know. I did. He should be here any moment. Stuck in traffic. Excuse me." He began to fumble into his pockets for his vial of pills.

Schurf looked at his watch with irritation, then signaled his stenographer to start setting up. As gear was unpacked, Schurf squeezed into a chair, blew his nose, opened his briefcase, and fixed his gaze on the wall clock. After readying the stenotype machine, the stenographer assembled a video camera on a tripod directly in front of Dr. Giardano. At the flick of a switch, a video spotlight glared directly into the doctor's face.

"What?" Giardano protested, squinting and recoiling from the bright, hot light. "Do you have to…?"

"Routine, doctor," said Schurf unsympathetically.

"Please turn it off until we start," Giardano insisted, looking even more cadaverously pale in the bright glow. The stenographer clicked it off, and began to tinker with the steno-type machine.

Miss White's voice came on the intercom. "Dr. Giardano, that call, from your brother-in-law, is on the line."

"OK, we'll take it." Giardano picked up the phone. "Tiny? Yes, they're here. OK, I'll put him on." He handed the phone to Schurf. "I promised my wife that my brother-in-law, an attorney, could talk to you before we started. Do you mind?"

Schurf scowled at the receiver before accepting it. "Ed Schurf here. Who's this? Tiny?" Schurf cupped his hand over the phone. "Your brother-in-law has some special vocal cords, doctor," referring to the peculiarly high-pitched voice on the other end of the line. "So what's up, Tiny. Gotta make it fast. We're running late already."

Schurf listened quietly for no more than twenty seconds, then interrupted. "Listen. No, you listen to me, Tiny. We appreciate your familial concern, but you are wasting your time! Whatever your so-called connections are, they don't interest or scare me a bit. There is no stopping this suit. Goodbye." He disconnected and handed the phone back to Giardano. "Where the hell did Tiny get his law degree?" he said scornfully. "Interrupting me like this. Now, if you please, if we can get on with the deposition."

Appearing stunned, Giardano pressed the intercom. "What's the word on the attorney?" he asked huskily.

"He just called," replied Miss White. "It was a bad connection—those mobile phones—but he said he's just a few blocks away from Metrocare."

"Mr. Schurf," said Giardano, dabbing his brow with a folded hand-kerchief. "My attorney is still delayed. But I want to get this over with. I have patients waiting, you know. Can we start without him?"

"That would be your call, doctor," said Schurf flatly.

"OK."

"Am I to understand that you are waiving your right to counsel, doctor?"

"Well, yes. I mean, until he gets here."

"Let the record show…" Schurf hesitated. "Turn on the video first."

The stenographer obeyed, and once again Dr. Giardano was in the glare of the video spotlight.

Schurf cleared his throat. "Let the record indicate that the defendant has voluntarily waived his right to counsel at the commencement of this proceeding. OK. Let's begin."

While the stenographer swore in Giardano, Schurf opened a file across his lap, rearranged a few documents, and started. "Let it be recorded that, in the case of Jerome W. Dranitzke vs Robert P. Giardano, M.D., this deposition commenced at 1:39 in his office of the 3rd floor of the Whittaker Building, address such and such West 53rd Street, on today's date, etc., etc. Doctor, would you please state your full name?"

"Dr. Robert Paul Giardano."

"Your occupation."

"Physician. Ophthalmologist. Eye surgeon."

"Your present position."

"I'm in private practice, and I am also the chief of the ophthalmology department here at Metrocare Hospital."

"Are you board-certified in ophthalmology?"

"Yes, of course."

"And the year of your taking the exam to become certified?"

"1972."

"1972. Long time ago."

"Well, yes," Giardano retorted. "But there are the continuing education requirements, every year, which I have met which you should ask about."

Schurf feigned surprise at the flustered protest. "My very next question. Doctor, would you summarize your training in medicine and ophthalmology?"

Giardano recited his medical training, beginning with his premedical studies at New York University. He repeatedly glanced at the wall above his desk to dozens of diplomas and awards which now climbed clear to the ceiling. When he had finished presenting his long and impressive credentials, his voice had acquired a tone of renewed self-confidence.

Schurf continued unphased. "Dr. Giardano, is it true that last year on June 18th you performed a corneal transplant on the left eye of a patient, one Mr. Jerome Dranitzke?"

"That is correct."

"And, for the record, you are aware of the fact that six weeks after the operation, the corneal graft tore loose, causing immediate and permanent blindness in that eye?"

"I know."

"And because the other, the right eye, is a lazy eye from birth, the patient for all intents and purposes is a blind person."

"Yes, but the left eye is blind because the patient fell post-op. It's in the emergency room records. The patient was drunk, fell, and hit the left eye."

"That is not our concern today, Dr. Giardano. Let's concentrate on the eye operation. Doctor, is it not true that the corneal graft you did tore loose because the sutures tore loose?"

"Yes."

"Doctor, isn't it true that you rushed when you placed the sutures during the operation?"

"What?" exclaimed Giardano, his mouth agape.

"Let me repeat the question. Isn't it true that you rushed when you placed the sutures during the operation?'

"Rushed? No, I didn't rush. What are you talking about?"

Schurf flipped ahead a few pages in his yellow legal pad. "Well, isn't it true that you said at that point in the operation, 'let's get these sutures in as fast as possible?'"

"What?" Giardano loosened his tie another inch.

"Doctor, we have testimony under oath from a nurse present in the room that you made that statement."

"I don't know exactly what I said, but now I—yes, I do. I do remember I didn't want to waste time because the patient had suddenly become restless and uncooperative. Alcoholic patients frequently respond idiosyncratically to anesthesia."

"We found no report of that in the operative record."

"I guess we didn't write it down because I solved the problem. I mean, I succeeded in putting in the sutures efficiently and properly. Christ, if we recorded every potential problem in the chart, we would spend our entire lives doing dictation."

"Doctor, in a court of law, if it's not in the record, it didn't happen."

"This is absurd. We have got to stop this, I mean, take a break—Jesus, it's hot in here," complained Giardano. He stood up, removed his white lab coat, and draped it over the back of his chair, then went to open the door and spoke to Miss White. "You've got to do something about this heat. Leave the door partly open, it might help. Send my lawyer in the instant he arrives. And please go get a pitcher of water, with ice, from down the hall."

Miss White nodded nervously, and left the room. Dr. Giardano returned to his desk chair and dug into one of the files on his desk. "Mr. Schurf, give me a second to find something, then we can we get on to the reasons why Mr. Dranitzke's eye needed a transplant. You know, the whole thing of the previous FERK operation for the herpes scar. Then we can get this all over with."

As Dr. Giardano fished into another file, Schurf shifted impatiently in his chair and watched him in disbelief. Moments later Miss White returned and placed the water pitcher and cups on his desk.

He tossed two more pills into his mouth and drank them down feverishly. "Miss White," he groaned, "I can't find the second FERK file—the yellow one—on Dranitzke."

"Isn't it in your first drawer?" she responded, promptly walking to the file cabinet and pulling out the top drawer. "Yes, here it is, doctor." She extracted the thick yellow file and carefully placed it on the corner of the desk.

"Thank you," Giardano said, relieved. "Now, Mr. Schurf, we can get to the most important part of all this." He started to open the file, and then hesitated. "Maybe we should wait a little longer. I think my attorney should be present from this point on."

Schurf looked at his notes, then at the stenographer, and back at the Giardano. "Well, actually, doctor, I have nothing more. I'm finished."

Giardano blinked. "Finished? What do you mean, finished? You haven't come to the most important part of all this, the FERK procedure that was done a month before I did the transplant."

"Doctor, I know that a procedure…"

"The FERK procedure," insisted Dr. Giardano.

"Alright, FERK procedure. And it was done by, let's see, by Doctor…"

"Royster. By Dr. Royster."

"Yes. Dr. Royster. But frankly that has no relevance in this case or this deposition."

Giardano leaned towards Schurf. "No relevance? Of course it has relevance! You must have it right there in your notes. Dr. Royster told you that the FERK procedure scarred and thinned the cornea, which then became infected because of the patients self-neglect. That is what led to the sutures failing!"

Outside, at the sound of Giardano's raised voice, Miss White moved silently to the edge of the open door and listened.

Schurf looked totally unimpressed. "Doctor. I took the deposition from Dr. Royster last week. He has testified under oath that after the procedure, the FERK operation, the cornea healed quite unremarkably. He made no mention of any complication relating to this FERK procedure."

"What! No mention?" gasped Giardano, jumping up from his chair and almost knocking over the camera tripod. "Turn it off! Dammit, turn off the TV!" he cried.

At Schurf's signal, the stenographer slid the camera to the side and switched it off.

"No mention?" Giardano shook his hands in the air. The FERK procedure weakened the corneal tissue. That's why the corneal transplant was vulnerable. When the Drantizke patient got drunk and fell down—Royster knows all this. Dear God, he must have told you!"

Schurf thrust forward a typewritten document. "Here, do you want to read the deposition?"

Giardano took the document and read it, moving his lips silently. Suddenly he stopped and clutched his upper left chest with his right hand.

He uttered one word.

"Pain."

Stumbling, he collapsed into his desk chair. "Nitro…"

With the two men staring stupidly at him, Giardano managed to wash down what was the last pill from the bottle. His face was turning a deep gray, and beads of diaphoretic sweat covered his forehead. He began to wretch with nausea, but nothing came up. Now his breath came shorter. A frothy spittle appeared at the corners of his mouth. Finally his eyes rolled up, and his limp body fell forward from chair to the floor.

Schurf and the stenographer exchanged looks of terror.

"Run!" blurted Schurf. "Get help."

The stenographer raced out of the room down the corridor to the main desk. "Quick!" he cried to the receptionist. "Do something! Come, it's the doctor, Dr. Giardano! He passed out!"

He and the receptionist sprinted down the main corridor, turned left, and ran into Giardano's office. There stood Schurf, frozen. On the floor lay Giardano, his face ashen, his body motionless. Next to him was Miss White, down on one knee and crying.

The receptionist took one look, grabbed the phone and dialed. "Code Gray, Whittaker, 3rd floor, Dr. Giardano's private office! Crash unit, stat! Hurry! Hurry!"

CHAPTER *Sixteen*

4:16 p.m.

"I'll call it. Time of death, 4:15," said the leader of the CPR team.

The resuscitation attempt had lasted an hour, long after Schurf had left and Miss White had been taken to the emergency room for a sedative. Gabe had rushed in at the end and took turns with Jack pumping the chest.

As stretcher bearers removed Giardano's body, and the team of nurses and doctors rolled their gear out the door, Jack and Gabe looked on helplessly. Finally they stood alone in the quiet, surrounded by Giardano's equipment.

Jack spotted the soft contact lens analyzer. "The contact lenses! And the disc!" he said.

They searched the entire suite and found Dr. Giardano's white coat hanging on the back of the Miss White's closet door. Searching one pocket, and reaching in the other, Jack fished out the 3.5 inch disc.

"Thank God," Jack sighed, staring at the 3.5 inch casing as if it were some newly unearthed religious talisman. He sat at the desk and dialed the the hospital administrator's office.

"Mr. Crantz's office," answered the secretary.

"This is Dr. Stegall. Is your boss in?"

"No, doctor, he's over at the Plaza Hotel in a meeting with Dr. Royster. Is there a message?"

"Yes. I must meet with Mr. Crantz in his office tomorrow morning at the earliest. It can't wait."

"How's 10 o'clock?"

"Fine."

Gabe looked alarmed. "Jack, you mean you're going to the administrator about Royster?"

"Precisely."

"But that's so dangerous! Why take on more than just the Dranitzke thing? I mean, you know, what you said about…"

"About not taking on doctors that are culpable but powerful?"

"Yes. It's so risky. Why?"

"Giardano was like a father…" Jack choked up.

Gabe leaned over and pressed her forehead to his shoulder. "Jack, I'm sorry…"

He blinked moisture from his eyes. "It's going to be OK. And this is going to be very, very interesting." He punched the computer's "ON" button.

Gabe grabbed a chair, squeezed next to him, and stared at the computer. "Let me help. What program does it use?"

"Bob used an older program, dBASE four. Should be pretty straightforward."

"Do we have a backup copy?"

He nodded. "Bob said Miss White keeps it." He keyed in to the dBASE dot prompt, slipped the data disc into the A drive, and after a pause the directory to the disc appeared.

They scanned the list of files. "Let's see," said Jack. "Yes, this must be it. FERK.DBF. That must be the existing FERK data." He keyed in for the file by typing "Use FERK.DBF," and a split-second later a table of data displayed on the screen.

Jack leaned forward and studied the screen. "Bingo! Look, Gabe! It's just like Giardano said." He scrolled downwards, pointing with his ballpoint. "See? 57 cases, and almost half have no data recorded after the first or second visit after the FERK procedure was done. And here— each of those cases ends with the letters L-T-F."

"Lost to follow," said Gabe.

"Lost to follow, yes, of course. So that's it. This file of data leads us to believe that those patients were lost to followup, that they stopped coming back for their examinations. Those must be the very cases that developed the corneal haze!"

"Yes, look, all of the remaining cases have excellent results. See? Here under the column headed 'cornea,' they all have the entry 'clear corneas, excellent healing, excellent clarity.'"

Jack nodded, eyes gleaming. "And guess what. These are exactly the cases that Royster is parading during the telecast."

"So the bad data?"

"It's got to be somewhere else on this disc where Bob transferred it. First we have to go back to the main file directory."

Jack keyed back to the directory, and read the remaining files aloud. "Glaucoma.DBF, Hyperop.DBF, Nearsgt.DBF, Presbyo.-DBF, and Retina.DBF. He must have dumped the data into one of these files. We'll just have to plough through them till we find it."

Jack keyed up the glaucoma file. It was a list of 100 patients with intraocular hypertension who had been treated with beta blocker eye drops to reduce the eye pressure. "Nothing here." Jack returned to the main file and keyed up the next entry, hyperopia. Again, no sign of the missing data.

"Maybe he put it on a different disc," said Gabe.

"No, no, he specifically said it was on this disc. Here, let's try near-sightedness. Maybe he parked it where it would be obvious."

Jack keyed it up, but after a few seconds, a blank screen appeared. Jack tried keying in "nearsightedness.DBF" and pressed the enter key: an empty screen appeared with the message, "No File Found."

"Well, scratch that. Must be on presbyopia or retinal detachment." Jack brought up the presbyopia file. There was nothing but 50 patients with an analysis of the power of their reading glasses compared to their age. Finally, he keyed in the retinal detachment file. Not a shred of data relating to the FERK study.

Jack began to feel uneasy. "What the hell?" he muttered. "I don't understand. Where is that data?" He re-keyed back to the file directory, then went to a help menu, then back to the FERK file, then back to the main menu. There was nothing to be found of the extracted data.

"Can I try?" asked Gabe.

"Sure." Jack slumped back in his chair.

"Let me try that nearsightedness file again," said Gabe. "I think there's one other key sequence you can use." Gabe went through an unusual key series, lifting Jack's hopes that the hidden data would appear on the screen at last. The computer seemed to strain, then paused, and finally once again the message appeared at the bottom of the screen: "No File Found."

Gabe frowned. "You would think that would be it, you know, nearsightedness, but it's not."

"I know. Damn it, that data is somewhere on this disc, but where?"

"Jack, do you think your partner made a mistake and erased it? Or, maybe Royster erased it somehow. Or maybe he wasn't telling the truth or something?"

"Gabe, I know he wasn't lying. Maybe he did accidentally erase it, or something happened to it. But I just know that these 26 patients who were supposedly lost to follow were actually the patients who got the corneal scarring." Jack stopped. "Wait a minute. Wait a big minute. Let's go back to the laundered data." Jack keyed it up and scanned the information. "Here it is. H.Q. That's got to be him."

"Who?"

"Herman Quimby, the homeless patient we saw in the emergency room. See, he's one of the cases that end with 'lost to follow.' It's got to be Quimby. Gabe, it may say he's lost to follow here, but he certainly isn't lost. He's right here in this hospital."

"Are you thinking what I'm thinking?"

Jack nodded. "I'm positive Quimby had the FERK procedure. He's the one person who can tell us how you go from having a lousy result in a surgical trial to being 'lost to follow'."

"And he may know something about the other 26 patients."

"Precisely. If we can't find the missing data, maybe we can find the missing patients. It's all we have to go on. He must have been admitted to the surgical service."

Jack picked up the phone and dialed the patient locator. "I'm sorry, doctor," came the reply, "but Mr. Quimby signed out against doctor's orders at five this morning."

Jack thanked her, hung up, and sagged back in his chair. "He's gone."

"Gone?"

"Left the hospital." Jack thought for a moment. "Gabe, I just bet he went straight back to Mercy Park. And I know who can help us find him."

"Your classmate doctor in the park?"

Jack nodded. "I'll find Peter Kinkaid, and he can lead me to Quimby."

"You're going into Mercy Park? Now?"

"Time's crucial."

"I'm coming too," Gabe said, reaching for her tote bag.

"I should go alone, and you can get the number of the Myopevue Contact Lens Company. I think they're down in Florida somewhere. Get their Distribution Department, and tell them we need to know about how many people in the New York City area use their minus 12 Myopevue soft lenses. No names for now, just a rough number. Don't say we're trying to narrow down the identify of a murdered woman. It might freak them out."

Gabe jotted down the information on a message pad.

"Let's meet for dinner, say, about seven?"

"Victor's Cafe on Columbus?"

"Perfect." Jack flicked off the computer and retrieved the disc. Exchanging his white coat for his suit jacket, he dropped the computer disc into the inside breast pocket and securely buttoned it. "Don't want to lose this, do we?"

They left the main building through the central entrance. Gabe peered across the entrance drive to Mercy Park. "Be careful," she called.

After letting an empty ambulance pass, Jack crossed the drive and entered the park. The sun, drooping close to the horizon beyond the Hudson, threw its few remaining rays into the park at a flat angle, bathing the gates in a soft glow and casting long shadows across the grounds. The park was practically deserted.

As Jack approached the central circle, he saw his classmate, standing behind a shirtless derelict, listening to his back with a stethoscope. Peter wore the same attire, the same threadbare doctor's lab coat, the same leather necklace. The fine head tremor was still evident.

Peter looked up, and did a double-take. "Jack?"

"Hello, Peter."

Peter's eyelid twitched noticeably. "Jack Stegall? Here in Mercy Park?"

Jack took two steps, then stopped when he realized his shadow stretching across the ground was joined by an even larger one. He turned. Behind him stood Bird, the mulatto who had accompanied Kinkaid the previous day. The fringed cowboy shirt had been replaced with a clean teeshirt. When their eyes met, Jack felt a lance of adrenal fear stab through him.

"No problem, Bird," said Peter. "He's a friend of mine."

The moment Bird hesitated, Peter ordered, "Go on. Do as I say." Bird shifted angry eyes onto Peter before disappearing.

Peter removed the stethoscope from his ears. "What brings Dr. Stegall to Mercy Park General Hospital?"

Jack, whose first concern was still Bird, glanced out of the tent before answering. "It's about the man you carried in yesterday, the one who was struck in the eye, Herman Quimby. He signed out of the emergency room. I have to find him."

Peter's eyebrows raised. "Quimby? I don't know, Jack. Quimby doesn't—he really doesn't want to have anything to do with Metrocare."

"It's important. I…" Jack's speech stalled.

Peter looked at Jack appraisingly. "Hey, man, you're upset. What is it?"

The words just fell out. "My partner. Dr. Giardano. He just died."

Peter continued to stare at Jack, then shifted his attention back to the shirtless man. "OK, friend, your lungs are clear now. Just be sure to keep better track of your medicines next time." After the man left, Peter walked over to Jack. "I'm sorry, but I don't get it. What are you doing here?"

Jack gazed downwards at the footworn grass. "It's complicated, Peter. A malpractice suit killed my partner—it involved some operations I think Quimby knows about. I've got to find him."

"Sounds like you really do." For a moment Peter studied Jack, then stuffed the stethoscope into his pocket. "Quimby is staying a few days with me."

Peter led the way out of the park to a cheap two-room apartment across Ninth Avenue. Quimby was sprawled asleep on a cot in the back. The bright spandex pants were the same, but the bloodied sweatshirt had been replaced with a heavy maroon pullover sweater.

Peter gave him a nudge. "Quimby. Wake up. You've got a visitor, man, the doctor who took care of your eye yesterday."

Quimby stirred, turned his head, and squinted at Jack with his unbandaged left eye. "Don't need no doctor," he mumbled.

Jack pulled up a chair next to him. "Listen, Quimby. Let me see that eye that was hit yesterday. It'll only take a second."

When the old man didn't seem to object, Jack unbandaged and examined the right eye. The swelling had subsided, and the eye appeared normal.

"Quimby, your right eye is doing fine. But I also want to ask you about your left eye."

Quimby turned away. "Ain't sayin' nothin'."

"Quimby, why won't you talk to me about your left eye?"

Silence.

Jack looked at Peter and back to Quimby. "I don't get it."

The old man frowned. "They said it was secret. Research stuff. We're not supposed to say nothin'. And I don't want no mo' trouble."

Jack decided to press. "Did Royster operate on your eye?"

"Don't want no mo' trouble." Quimby sat up and started to put on muddy jogging shoes as if to leave.

"Is it the men who beat you up? Who was behind it?"

Peter intervened. "C'mon, oldtimer, talk to the doctor. He's a friend. He's already helped you. He needs your help."

Quimby looked down at the ground, picking wax from his ear. Finally he looked up at Peter. "Gotta a cigarette, doc?"

The cigarette was produced and lit. Quimby took a short puff. The smoke seemed to irritate his left eye. "OK," he finally said. "He operated. Yeah."

"What did he do?" asked Jack.

"He did the big electron gizmo operation on my bad eye."

"Why did you stop going back afterwards?"

"Hey, man, I didn't stop," said Quimby, taking another puff. "Royster told us we didn't have to come back."

"Us? How do you mean, us?"

"I mean, you know, a whole bunch of us had that electronic thing done. Royster paid us $100 to go through with it, and then $20 for each time we come back to have it checked. But then a lot of us was told not to come back no mo' and…"

Jack cut him off. "Wait, Mr. Quimby, let's back up. How come so many of you out in the park became Royster's patients to begin with?"

Quimby looked at Peter for reassurance.

"It's OK," said Peter. "Tell him what you know."

"He checked all of us down at the shelter, hell, last year sometime."

"The shelter, the one down on 49th that closed down?" Jack asked. It was all starting to make sense.

"Yeah. Royster came down there, hell, every day for a week, and picked out the ones who had these damned herpes scars like me. Then he paid us to have the operation, and then later he told some of us not to come back no mo'. Except to JCG."

"JCG? What's JCG?"

"You know, the hospital, Jersey City General. Royster's people, you know, set us all up with Welfare and Medicare and whatnot over in Jersey City, ya understand what I'm sayin'? Shit, we all got fed, clothed, got doctors, social workers, the works. I seen some of the other guys over there comin' and goin' all the time."

"Why did you come back," Jack asked.

"I like it in Mercy Park." Quimby looked up at Jack and Peter. "That's where I belong, ya know what I'm sayin'? So I come back."

"So that's it," Jack said softly to himself.

CHAPTER *Seventeen*

Fifteen minutes later Jack arrived at Victor's Cafe and took a table at the end of the stretch of windows looking out on Columbus Avenue. He ordered a whiskey for himself, wine and paella for two, then looked glumly out on the West Side evening street life. The seemingly carefree dinner-goers and passersby made him feel he was of another planet, alone, distraught. Jack's drink and Gabe arrived at the same time.

"Hi," said Jack, forcing a smile as he rose to greet her. "Drink?"

She asked for a wine spritzer and sat down opposite him. "Are you all right, Jack?" She was in a silk blouse, jacket, and stirrup pants, and looked lovelier than ever. The vision of her smiling at him across the white table cloth, and the first taste of whiskey warming his throat made the inner pain lift.

"I'm OK."

"I've been so worried. Mercy Park. Did you get any more information?"

"Yes. But did you get through to the Myopevue people?"

"Yes." Gabe pulled a sheet of notes from her purse. "It doesn't look to good. They said that 4863 people wear those lenses. That includes all of New York City and parts of New Jersey, Long Island, and Connecticut."

"It's a needle in the haystack," Jack said.

"Right. What did you learn in the park?"

In hushed tones, Jack told her Quimby's entire story. When he finished, they both sipped their drinks in contemplation.

"Despicable," Gabe said finally. "Absolutely dispicable. I am so sorry, Jack. What now?"

"I still think there is a high enough 'lost to follow' percentage to question the remaining data. It's like the study is half missing. Anybody with any common sense should see that. And there could be more to it, like Giardano said."

"Are you still going to meet the administrator?"

"It's all I've got right now."

"But will he listen? Jack, I think it's going to be so hard for anybody to stop the TV program."

"I know."

"If he doesn't listen, what will you do?"

Jack hesitated. "I'm going to call the Food and Drug Administration in Washington."

"The FDA? Jack, what will Metrocare and the Royster people do to you?"

"Whatever happens, I can always re-establish a practice elsewhere in Manhattan. I still have my practice, my home."

Gabe squeezed his hand. "And me."

The waiter brought the heaping portions of paella and served the split of white wine. They touched their glasses and drank. Hungerless, he watched Gabe pick at her food, then pushed his plate to the side and gazed back onto Columbus Avenue. "I think the numbness is starting to wear off about Giardano's death. I can't get over it. I knew him for over 5 years."

"Has anybody reached his wife yet?"

"No. I don't think she gets back from Italy until tomorrow evening."

Jack gazed out the window at the sidewalk's evening crowds, lost in gloom.

"Let's go," said Gabe.

"Hm?" He barely heard her.

"C'mon, let's go."

"OK. I left my car down at Metrocare. We have to pick it up first."

They taxied down to the doctor's garage, recovered his silver Porsche, and soon were driving back to the Dakota. Gabe sat close to him but neither spoke; both were completely talked out. They arrived, Jack parked in the underground garage, and, holding hands, the two proceeded to his apartment. Once inside, Gabe immediately took his hand, led him to the bedroom, and sat him on the edge of the bed.

"I'll be right back," she said.

Jack's despondency yielded to anticipation.

CHAPTER *Eighteen*

WEDNESDAY, 9:04 a.m.

Next morning the sun was pushing its way through a light drizzle when Jack dropped Gabe off at her apartment and drove on to Metrocare where he headed straight for the second floor to Hospital Administration. Entering the new and unfamiliar office complex, he hesitated until a helpful receptionist pointed the way past the clerical offices to Crantz's office suite in the rear.

"Good morning. Your name please?" asked the private secretary.

"I'm Dr. Stegall. I have an appointment with Mr. Crantz at 9:30." Jack regarded the young, tastefully dressed woman. She wore a "METRO-CARE—FIRST IN VISION" button and, sitting idly behind a neat, polished desk, looked as if she'd just stepped from a sleek magazine ad for office furnishings. At the corner of the desk a single pink carnation stood in a small crystal vase.

"Lucky you," Jack said. "No managed care hassles or upset patients. If my secretary saw this, she would flip."

"Oh, yes, Miss White. I was talking with her this morning. She sounds very nice." The secretary glanced at a schedule. "Mr. Crantz is running a little late. Won't you have a seat? May I get you coffee, doctor?"

"Thank you," said Jack, wondering why administration would be talking to Miss White. Must be concerning Giardano's death, he figured.

The secretary rose and walked to a silver coffee service alongside her desk. As she filled one of the imported china cups, Jack examined the lavish furnishings and decorations of the reception area. Plush carpeting and linen wallpaper set off the assortment of fine antiques, collectors' art, and down-filled, upholstered chairs. The divan he sat on was in soft chenille. He remembered how, during his intern days, the administration department was located in the basement in cramped offices not far from the boiler room. Now—ever since the hospital chain took over—administration had the best site in the hospital to make its new image of affluent corporate success unmistakable.

The secretary served his coffee. Jack sipped it, then opened his briefcase to take a last look at the computer disc with the FERK data. Almost 50% lost to follow, he thought. Obviously unacceptable, but would Crantz agree? Jack looked up at the secretary, who smiled back. He wondered if Crantz would be smiling after being told to cancel the FERK operation. He felt a wave of nausea.

The administrator's door suddenly opened and Crantz, wearing a dark pin-striped suit, stepped out. "Dr. Stegall, good to see you. Come in, come in. Sorry to keep you waiting."

After a handshake, Jack followed Crantz into the spacious office and took a seat in one of the two leather-upholstered wingbacked chairs opposite the administrator's oversized oak desk. Jack quickly inventoried the room—the large oval conference table, the built-in wetbar, the faux-finished wall covered with shiny awards and certificates of merit, the small, Sheraton table in the corner with its collection of Baccarat figurines.

Crantz sat down behind his desk, whirled in his chair to pull a file from his credenza, turned around, and lit a cigar.

"Smoke?"

"No thanks."

"Comfortable, Jack? Get you something? Coffee?"

Jack declined.

Crantz produced a handkerchief and began to fold it in preparation. "Terrible, terrible thing about Dr. Giardano. I wanted to reach Mrs. Giardano, but I understand she's returning from a trip abroad. Terrible thing. Last time we had a physician die in the hospital, I believe, was over 7 years ago." Crantz nervously shifted some papers on his desk, and adjusted his hefty frame in the chair. "So you wanted to talk to me about the FERK thing?"

"I'll come right to the point," said Jack. "Yesterday just before Dr. Giardano died," he had to pause for a moment to control a surge of grief, "we had a discussion of the latest data. He told me it looked bad, very bad, and didn't meet the requirements of the protocol to move ahead. He was going to see you yesterday to call a moratorium on the procedure and…"

Crantz held up his hands to interrupt. "Jack, I have to stop you right there, right there." He pressed down his intercom and asked, "Is Dr. Royster here yet?"

"Royster!" blurted Jack, jumping to his feet. "Did you tell him I was meeting with you?"

Crantz didn't look up, but instead reached for a second file in his aluminum briefcase. He faced Jack again with an anxious look. "Dr. Stegall, you better believe I want Royster to be here when you talk about canning the FERK operation. Do you realize how much work, how much publicity has gone into this, just into the production we have planned for tomorrow?"

The intercom buzzed. "Dr. Royster is here."

"Show him in," said Crantz.

Royster entered, warmly greeted Crantz, then turned to Jack and gave him a perfunctory pat on the shoulder. "Jack, how are you? Awful thing about Bob Giardano."

Fists clenched, his face reddening, Jack acknowledged the insincere remark with a curt nod and sat down. Royster took the remaining chair, and brushed a fleck of lint from the dark blue Italian suit which looked even more expensive than the one he'd worn at the television rehearsal. The hand-tooled cowboy boots looked shinier.

Crantz wiped the first beads of perspiration from his forehead. "Doctors, we're all very upset, very grieved about the sudden and tragic loss of Dr. Giardano. But let's get to the point of this right away. Dr. Stegall, please continue."

Jack looked at the administrator, then at Royster, straining to grasp what they might have said to each other since Jack had scheduled the meeting. There was no choice but to forge ahead. As he reached for his briefcase, he guaged the tightrope he would have to walk. He needed strong ammunition, but he couldn't go too far. He would look foolish if he mentioned data hidden on a disc and ludicrous if he recounted the story of a homeless alcoholic in Mercy Park. He certainly couldn't bring up story of the murdered woman, or any idea that there were complications worse than corneal scarring. All he could safely discuss was the high percentage of cases attributed to "lost to follow."

Jack opened his briefcase and removed the disc. "Just before Dr. Giardano died yesterday, he showed me this disc which contains the data for the clinical trials of FERK. As you well know, Dr. Royster, this disc is a duplicate of the one you possess. I am here this morning, Mr. Crantz, to tell you what Dr. Giardano would have told you, that is, that there is an extremely high rate of patients who were lost to follow-up early in their post-operative period. Many of these lost patients could have had complications which didn't appear in the patients who remained. I believe, as Dr. Giardano did, that any and all FERK operations should be halted until these other patients can be tracked down and examined. It's the safe and prudent thing to do, Mr. Crantz." Jack pointed to the desktop computer on his desk. "I'd like to display this data for you to show you the high rate of lost patients."

Crantz started to speak, but Royster interrupted. "Dr. Stegall," he said with a condescending drawl, "no need to waste our time trudging through the complicated FERK data on a computer terminal. I happen to have the data neatly printed out and analyzed, so if I may." Royster opened his briefcase and extracted a neatly bound report entitled, "FERK—Clinical Trials, Phase II." He opened it to the final page and laid it in front of Crantz. "You see, Emmet, almost all of the eyes operated on showed perfect post-operative healing. As in all studies, there was a certain percentage of patients lost to follow, but statistics will show that the remaining patient population is sufficient to rely on."

"The lost to follow patients were almost 50% of the total," Jack blurted.

"Not an uncommon rate in studies of this kind," said Royster cooly.

"You can't be serious," insisted Jack. "I..."

"Gentlemen, gentleman," interrupted Crantz, standing up and raising his hands for silence. "I am not a doctor. I am not an ophthalmologist. But Jack, a certain rate of lost patients doesn't sound so bad to me."

"Exactly," said Royster. "And what if there is a small risk? No new procedure is without its risks, without its drawbacks." He rose from his chair, walked to the window, and pulled up the blinds, causing everyone to squint in the sudden flood of sunlight into the room. "Anybody is a fool not to realize that this procedure holds the promise of curing near-sightedness for millions upon millions of people simply with the touch of a computer button."

"I'm aware of that," answered Jack undaunted, looking past Royster directly at Crantz. "But I am also fully aware of the fact that for every 1% of failure of this procedure, not just one patient tomorrow, but literally thousands of people could be blinded."

"Dr. Stegall," Royster's voice tightened. "This is all becoming a little tiresome. You're entitled to your opinion, and now you should bow out. The bottom line here is that the FDA has accepted our work and approved FERK for normal myopes."

"Did you tell them about the high rate of patients lost to follow?"

A confident smile appeared on Royster's face. Suddenly Jack remembered the photograph in Royster's office showing the surgeon shaking hands with the FDA director. Maybe he had sold the official the same bill of goods.

Jack turned to the administrator. "Mr. Crantz, I request you give my opinion special consideration. I have been an alternate for the Eye Research Committee, and with Dr. Giardano's death, I should now be joining the committee automatically."

His handkerchief soaked, Crantz produced a fresh one and cleared his throat. "Well, Dr. Stegall, that issue was considered earlier, and Dr. Benton, the newly added alternate, has been, uh, selected."

Jack sprang from his chair. "What? Benton? What does Benton know about this?"

"Dr. Benton," Royster retorted, "has extensive experience with laser and laser technologies."

Jack glared at his opponent. "This has nothing to do with his kind of lasers, and you know it. He has no corneal experience."

Crantz started to speak, but was cut off by Royster again. "You're entitled to your opinion, Dr. Stegall." He picked up his briefcase and looked at his Patek Phillipe. "I'm late." He turned as if to leave, then turned back. "Oh, I almost forgot. The computer disc you brought in today, Stegall. Clearly you have no use for it, and it correctly belongs with the proper authorities. Correct, Emmet?"

"He's right," answered Crantz hoarsely. "The disc is no longer any concern of yours. I'll take it now, Dr. Stegall." The administrator looked as if he would hide behind his handkerchief if he could.

Jack handed the disc over. Crantz slipped it into the shallow inside pocket of his aluminum briefcase and snapped it shut. "Now, Jack, I want you to listen to…"

Jack interrupted. "No, you listen to me. Consider yourselves warned."

Royster spoke solemnly. "Dr. Stegall, if you have any misguided ideas of going above our heads, you can forget them. Crantz and I contacted your secretary Miss White this morning, and appropriately recovered this backup copy of Giardano's disc." He removed a second disc from his jacket pocket. "It too, belongs with us. Good day, gentleman." He walked out the door.

Jack felt the blood drain from his head.

Crantz flopped back in his chair. "Dr. Stegall, you know with Dr. Giardano gone we are officially looking for his replacement as chief of the department. Frankly, you and Royster are the only people qualified for the job that I, for one, would endorse. It's a bad time to be rocking the boat. Look, let's be a team. Why don't you be my guest at the FERK Benefit Ball tonight at the Plaza Hotel? Their parent company, Globe International, is putting it on. I hear with all the money they put into it, it's going to be some helluva bash. Grand Ballroom, music, dancing, celebrities, the works."

Jack started to say, "Hell, no."

"Look," said Crantz, "you don't have to make up your mind now. I'll have my secretary get all the details to your office, and add your name to the guest list. Bring a guest."

As Crantz escorted him to the door, Jack looked back at the aluminum briefcase on Crantz's desk. The edge of the disc was visible above the pocket where Crantz had placed it.

CHAPTER *Nineteen*

Jack took the stairs to the first floor and headed straight for medical records, not to dictate or sign any charts, but to find privacy to call Gabe. Once there, he took an unoccupied dictation booth at the far end of the room and placed a call to her through the page operator. A minute later Gabe called back.

"Where are you?" asked Jack. The despair came through in his voice.

"I'm at my plastic surgery lecture in the surgery conference theatre. Jack, how did it go? Did Mr. Crantz agree with you?"

Jack started to tell Gabe the details of the disastrous meeting, when several medical residents strode into the record room and took booths close by.

"Gabe, I can't talk now—let's just say the meeting was not a huge success. Listen, I have to get away from all of this, get the hell out of the hospital."

"But your office…"

"I'll get coverage, and Miss White is handling all the calls."

"Sure," said Gabe. "I've got a great idea. The Circle Line around Manhattan."

"No, that's too…"

"Jack, you have to relieve your mind of all of this."

"You really want to go yourself?"

"Sure. Where you go, I go, remember?" said Gabe warmly. "Jack, I miss you."

"I miss you the same, Gabe." He was interrupted as another doctor took the booth next to his. "The Circle Line?"

"Terrific."

"Two-thirty in front of the ticket booth."

"See you there."

Jack left the hospital, drove to the Dakota to change into khakis and a warm sweater, then caught a cab for the Circle Line Pier at 42nd and 12th. The cab driver was friendly, talkative, and an overcast sky was rapidly giving way to cumulous clouds in an azure sky. By the time the pier came into view, Jack's rage at Royster, Crantz, and Metrocare Hospital had eased in anticipation of an afternoon with Gabe on the water in the warm April sun.

She was clad in stone-washed jeans and a navy blue pullover and waiting patiently at the ticket booth when Jack arrived. He took her in his arms and they kissed.

"I already bought the tickets," she said brightly. "Let's go—the boat's about to leave."

With a few other latecomers, they raced up the ramp to the 400-passenger tourboat. As soon as they boarded, the gangway was pulled in and the lines tossed free. Jack took Gabe's arm and led the way to the bow. Standing at the rail, they watched as the vessel, its engines rumbling into reverse, pulled them out into the Hudson, and then turned southwards towards the New York Harbor.

By now, the presence of Gabe and the sights and sounds of the river allowed Jack to take his mind off of the crisis at Metrocare Hospital for the first time in three days. It was only when Gabe asked that he told her about the meeting with Crantz.

"It couldn't have gone worse," Jack muttered. He turned his back to the rail and peered across the river at the New Jersey shoreline. "Royster owns Crantz. Royster showed up and claimed the FDA accepted the high number of 'lost to follow' patients. I had to hand over Giardano's data disc."

"But the backup."

Jack winced. "They'd already confiscated the backup from Miss White."

"Oh no!"

Jack nodded.

"And that was it?"

"That was it. Except my consolation prize was Crantz inviting me to the FERK Benefit Ball at the Plaza tonight. What a joke." Jack felt dejection returning.

"Oh, Jack, let's go! You and I both know they're lying about FERK. Something may crop up. What do we have to lose?"

"But what do we hope to gain? No thanks, Gabe. It's just not my problem anymore." He turned and looked off over the water, face hardened. The fingernail dug in.

"It's that snake, Royster, isn't it? How he treated you. The sleaze."

"Partly that. And what he's doing to people, to our profession. But he wins and the game's over. Except his lying about the Dranitzke case, but I don't believe the suit will stand. If it does, Giardano's life insurance will be enough to protect his widow and the office. Anyway, I'm out of it."

Gabe shrugged, and they both fell silent as they listened to the tour announcer describe the sights and history as the boat passed the southern tip of Manhattan.

"And on your right, the coastline of Hudson County, New Jersey," came the announcers tinny voice.

Jack turned. "Hudson County! Gabe, Giardano said the woman who was killed said something about New Jersey. Her pin said H C N A. That could mean Hudson County Nurse's Association. Most counties have one."

Gabe studied the shoreline. "It seems possible to me. Do you have your phone?"

Jack produced his cellular, and moments later Gabe was talking to Myopevue. Gabe asked them to rerun their minus 12 database specifically for Hudson County, New Jersey.

"They'll call back in a few minutes," she told Jack.

The vessel entered the great harbor below where a salty breeze turned the water to a light chop, and seagulls swirled and screamed about their boat and the passing tugboats, Jack's mood began to lift, and by the time they had passed the Statue of Liberty, he felt reinvigorated. Thinking back to Metrocare, he found himself wishing the boat would continue to sail on, south, to some place of harmony, some place away from all of the mess.

When his phone beeped, he handed it to Gabe.

"Yes, how many?" Gabe jotted the number on her tour ticket, said goodbye, and looked at Jack. "Only 118 people in Hudson County."

"It's a long shot." He took the phone and called his office.

His secretary sounded fatigued. "Miss White, I would like you to get the number of the Hudson County Police, then call the Myopevue Company in Florida, and ask them to fax the 118 names on their list. If the police come up with anything, tell them to call me."

Jack hung up. "It's worth a try."

When the wind grew chilly, he and Gabe walked to the stern, sat on one of the observation benches, and warmed themselves in the sun. By the time the vessel completed its arc through the harbor and was steaming up the East River, he and Gabe were deep in conversation again, this time about the architectural wonders of East Manhattan. They had passed beneath the Brooklyn and 59th Street Bridges, and were nearing Yankee Stadium, when Gabe's beeper sounded. Jack gave her his pocket flip-phone, and she dialed the number.

"Gabe, where are you?" came Maria's voice. "I've been dying to talk to you." The weak connection faded in and out.

Gabe hugged Jack tightly as she spoke into the thin receiver. "Jack and I are taking the afternoon off, you know, after what happened yesterday. What's with you, Maria? You just left the lecture and disappeared."

"I am so psyched. I'm calling from the Plaza. I'm going to the FERK Benefit Ball tonight!"

"You're going to the Ball?" asked Gabe, astonished.

"Yes, and something very exciting is going to happen."

"What do you mean?"

"I'm dying to tell you, but it's supposed to remain top secret until tonight. Let's just say that someone dropped out of tomorrow's operation." Once again static filled the line, breaking the connection completely.

CHAPTER *Twenty*

6:58 p.m.

The black-uniformed, white-hatted doorman, gold shoulder epaulets, tassels, and taxi whistle glimmering in the headlights, efficiently opened the passenger door, offered his white-gloved hand to Gabe, and queried, "Hospital Ball?"

"That's us," answered Gabe, straightening her sleek blue evening dress as she stepped onto the sidewalk.

"Grand Ballroom," said the doorman.

"Which way?" asked Jack emerging from the car in a black tuxedo. He'd only visited the Plaza once before, a hospital departmental cocktail party held in one of the more diminutive banquet rooms. The Grand Ballroom had eluded him entirely.

"Inside, follow the signs to your left, Grand Ballroom marble staircase up," answered the doorman impatiently as he abandoned Jack in favor of the stretch limos bringing in a fresh wave of arrivals.

Handing the keys to his Porsche to a parking valet, Jack took Gabe's arm, and together they ascended the red-carpeted steps, passed between marble pillars and 8-foot cast-bronze Vanderbilt sentry lamps, and entered the hotel's brass revolving doorway. Ignoring the marbled opulence surrounding them, they moved swiftly through the mirrored foyer, stepped through the giant Palladian French doors in front of the

Palm Court, and turned left down the corridor leading to the Ballroom stairway.

Ascending the balustraded marble staircase, they found themselves caught in a steady stream of other arriving ball-goers. Looking down to avoid direct eye contact, Jack at first became aware of the attire—the swishing boutique-bought designer dresses, the expensive black tuxedos, the fine, Italian leather shoes pacing up the carpeted steps. He shifted his gaze to the level of the watches and jewelry—solid-gold Ebel's, Rolexes, Guccis, Cartier diamond bracelets, Tiffany emerald and ruby bracelets, rings with diamonds the size of fingertips. Venturing to eye-level, Jack scrutinized the face-lifted, tanned, salon-pampered complexions, the flawless makeup, the haute-couture hairstyles, the upward chins. Jack pulled Gabe tight to his side and whispered, "Who said the rich were different than the rest of us? How ridiculous."

"Yeah, sure," Gabe whispered back. "And did you see that lady ahead with the diamond-studded tiara? Wow!"

Swept upwards by the dazzling horde, Jack and Gabe reached the Terrace Level's gilded Ballroom Foyer. Clustering before the triple sets of mirrored doors leading to the Ballroom, the other guests sprang to life with a flurry of heady greetings and air kisses.

The moment Jack and Gabe set foot inside, Jack felt a tap on the shoulder. It was Crantz, attired in an ill-fitting tuxedo, a tumbler of scotch in one hand, the damp handkerchief in the other.

"Dr. Stegall. I'm so glad you decided to come," Crantz grinned, producing one of a dozen last minute invitations.

"Thank you," replied Jack. "This is Gabe Richards."

"A pleasure to meet you," Crantz muttered. "Now don't take another step before you get buttoned." He turned and walked over to the rear table where he'd been sitting. There lay his aluminum briefcase, open and brimming with bags of Metrocare buttons. Jack's eyes riveted onto the briefcase—Giardano's computer disc was still securely tucked in the back pocket.

Crantz removed two buttons, rushed back to Jack and Gabe and offered to pin them on.

"That's OK." Jack took the buttons in his hand. "We'll put them on later."

"That reminds me." He dug into his pants pocket and pulled out a small blue envelope. "Here are my tickets for the late night breakfast in the Terrace Room." He poked the envelope in Gabe's hand. "You two go. I leave early for my flight."

"And miss the big TV show?" Jack said.

"Oh, we won't miss it. It's the Metrocare stockholders meeting in Chicago. We'll all watch the telecast." Without excusing himself, Crantz deserted Jack and Gabe to intercept a wealthy-looking couple at the entrance.

An usher appeared, and Jack handed him the invitation.

"That's the last table on the right."

Jack wasn't surprised they would be placed far in the back, banished among the anonymous. But he preferred it that way, to be on the sidelines, more an observer than a participant. The usher escorted them to the table. The remaining 6 table guests hadn't arrived yet, so Jack and Gabe chose the 2 chairs facing the dance floor and stage. Before sitting, both scanned the room.

"I don't see her," said Jack.

"Where the heck are you, Maria Sanchez?" Gabe said.

Gabe sat down, but Jack remained standing to observe the scene. The marble floors and columns, gilded porticos, and ornate trim were more stunning than anything he'd imagined about the famous room. The guests were seated at large, elaborately set, flower-laden dinner tables, and on the stage at the far end a 20-piece orchestra was already in the full swing with a rendition of Glenn Miller's "Pennsylvania 6-5000". In front of the orchestra stood three microphones. Jack became aware of a flickering motion high above his head and looked up at the center of the ceiling. Suspended mid-air by thin cables from the rotary shaft was a giant model of the FERK machine.

After a few minutes Royster, dressed in an all silk burgundy tuxedo, bounded up the side steps and took over the microphone.

There was long applause until he raised his hands to hush the crowd. "Good evening, ladies and gentleman. Welcome to the first of what will be an annual event, to celebrate our laser program, and to entertain you, our most loyal supporters. As you know, almost every individual here tonight has made at least a $250,000 investment in our limited partnership to capitalize FERK's new international subsidiary, the division which will distribute the FERK machines and training all over the world to the millions upon millions of nearsighted who wish to throw away their glasses forever. Good news. The FDA has us pre-market approval!"

The ballroom shook with applause and cries of "bravo." Royster had to ask for quiet 3 times before the outburst subsided.

"So we have a little surprise for you," Royster continued. "It's literally under your seats—the new Prospectus on our offering!"

Jack and Gabe watched as everyone eagerly pawed the underside of their chairs, came up with the Prospectus tied in a scroll with gold ribbon, and perused it with "ooohs" and "aahs." Finally, Jack begrudingly retrieved the one beneath his chair and held it out for himself and Gabe to read.

"It's their IPO!" said Gabe.

"Yeah, look, 20 million shares of common stock."

"They were going public all along!" Gabe whispered.

Jack nodded in contempt as his eyes searched the porticos for Maria. "You're right, Gabe. Keep looking."

"But there's more," said Royster. "Tonight you get the unique opportunity of saying hello to the lucky person who will have the operation tomorrow."

As the crowd jabbered with anticipation, Royster took the mike from the stand and walked to the edge of the stage. "Time for introductions. Before bringing up my distinguished collaborators from Japan and Russia, there are many notable Americans with us tonight, and I'd like them to take a bow."

More spotlights swung from portico to portico as celebrities took turns standing and waving to the applauding guests. Royster had finished with several retired sports figures, and was moving on to a few aging movie stars when Jack's beeper sounded. He checked the telephone number on the digital display, expecting it to be the familiar number of the hospital. It was completely different.

"718-321-5124? What the hell is that?" Jack wondered aloud.

"718-321. That's a Queens exchange, isn't it?" Gabe said.

"Queens. I better take it. Be right back."

Jack left the ballroom and quickly located the bank of telephones off the foyer. They were all in use. He walked to a far corner, removed his Motorola pocket phone from his inside pocket, and dialed. After two rings, a high pitched voice with a heavy Italian accent answered. "Stegall?"

"Yeah, this is Dr. Stegall. Who's this?" Jack was beginning to feel annoyed.

"This is Tiny, Dr. Stegall. I'm Bob Giardano's brother-in-law. Where are you, doctor?"

"At the Plaza Hotel. I assume you're calling about funeral arrangements for Bob?"

"Not exactly, not right now. Dr. Stegall, I'm calling from International Arrivals at Kennedy Airport. Mrs. Giardano just flew in, and we're driving her into Manhattan. She must meet you tonight."

"Tonight? But it's so late. Suppose I call her instead, later at…"

"Dr. Stegall, this won't wait. It's about the new eye procedure."

"What?"

"We can't explain now. A family limousine will pick you up at the Plaza in exactly ten minutes."

"I don't know, Mr., Mr…"

"Carbono."

"Mr. Carbono. I'm sure Mrs. Giardano is grief-stricken, and I share that grief, but I don't think that tonight…"

"After Mrs. Giardano talks to you, you'll understand. We'll have you back at the Plaza in an hour. Pick you up in 10 minutes." There was a click, and silence.

CHAPTER *Twenty-one*

The black limousine was already waiting at the curb when Jack emerged from the 5th Avenue entrance. "Dr. Stegall?" called the burly chauffeur. His cheaply dyed hair was black as his suit.

"Right. Stegall."

The chauffeur opened the rear door, Jack jumped in, and moments later the limousine was headed south on 5th. "Where are we going?" Jack asked.

"Little Italy."

Five miles to the south on Grant Street the chauffeur was escorting Jack into Giotti's Restaurant, a small, little-noticed Italian establishment squeezed into the row of well-known Italian dining landmarks between Mulberry and Bowery. Jack was whisked past the few patrons still finishing their meals in the shadowy front dining room and shown to a corner table in the secluded rear section.

Of the six people seated there, Mrs. Giardano was the first to attract Jack's attention, not so much that he identified her small features, but that she was wearing full mourning attire, including a fine lace black veil which hung gracefully over the upper half of her face. About to extend his condolences, he stopped short. Sitting opposite her was Ed Schurf. Jack almost didn't recognize him—he looked terrified and had a swollen bruise under his left eye. Flanking Schurf were two hefty men wearing dark suits and wide silk ties.

A man next to Mrs. Giardano stood up. He was big, bigger than Schurf, bigger than the two seated next to Schurf. The last time Jack had seen anyone so enormous was when he'd operated on the traumatic cataract of a defensive tackle for the New York Jets. The towering man extended his hand. "Hello, Dr. Stegall. I wish to thank you for coming down on such short notice. I am Tiny Carbono."

The high pitched voice went with the name Tiny, but name and body were exact opposites. This Tiny was huge.

"Won't you have a seat." Tiny pointed at a chair the chauffeur pulled up to the table. Jack sat down, speechless.

Mrs. Giardano began by thanking him for his expressions of sympathy. "You were so loved by my husband," she went on. "I'm sorry we have to meet under these circumstances."

Tiny patted his sister on the hand. "Doctor, I'll come right to the point. Upon her return to Kennedy Airport this evening, Mrs. Giardano informed me, as her brother and as an attorney, of certain facts pertaining to the FERK surgical trials, which until now, until Dr. Giardano's death, she had no choice but to conceal. The bottom line is, Dr. David Royster has committed scientific fraud and perjury to give the appearance that his operation works."

"This is what I found out just yesterday," Jack said.

Mrs. Giardano spoke in lowered tones. "A few weeks ago I noticed that Bob was acting strangely and seemed unhappy. I pressed him and finally he admitted that Royster had persuaded him to destroy all of the bad research data on FERK. I begged him to put an end to it. Bob wouldn't listen. He said it was just a device to avoid red tape."

Jack looked at Tiny and back at Mrs. Giardano. "That's precisely what Bob told me. And Royster betrayed him."

"Betrayed him in many ways," said Mrs. Giardano. "Mister Schurf here has provided my brother with the details. Royster caused his death, and now I've been informed that Royster plans to go ahead with this dangerous surgery. Jack, that is why I have called you here. Bob's reputation, everything he believed in, everything he worked for his whole life, Royster is about to drag down and destroy. I want Royster…" her voice choked with rage.

"Stopped." Tiny finished the sentence.

"Yes, stopped," Mrs. Giardano resumed quietly. "And we know you can stop him, if you're willing."

Though the other tables were unoccupied, Jack leaned forward and spoke in a hushed voice. "More willing than you can imagine, Mrs. Giardano. But there's something you don't realize. Dr. Giardano told me he never destroyed the data, but instead moved it somewhere else on the computer disc. I searched and searched that disc, but the incriminating data was nowhere to be found. It must be lost, permanently."

"The data isn't lost," said Tiny.

"It's not?" Jack stared at Tiny in amazement. "What do you mean, not lost?"

Tiny left that question to Mrs. Giardano, who answered it with a tone of vengeance. "My husband was ethical, a good man, right down to his bones. Like you said, Royster told him to destroy the bad data, and Bob couldn't do it. But he didn't just move it. That would have been too risky. Royster may have found it. So he hid it. He hid it good."

Jack looked at Tiny and back at the widow. "Where?"

"Right on the disc."

"On the disc? That can't be. I searched every single file. It just wasn't there."

Beneath the veil, a faint smile formed. "My husband was getting pretty good with computers. He has the data hidden in a file inside another file. You have to know where to look, and you have to know the instructions to get to the data. But it's on the disc." She opened her purse, and produced a small, sealed yellow envelope. "After he hid it, he gave me this envelope. He said that he and I were the only ones who knew the data was hidden on the disc, and that, if anything should ever happen to him, I should have the instructions just in case. You knew how he always…," there was a catch in her voice, "…he tried to think of everything."

"We knew we could count on you, Dr. Stegall," said Tiny, "to help us put a stop to this FERK racket, and give Royster what's coming to him. We've discussed the matter at length with Mr. Schurf here. He informed us that possession of the disc passed from Dr. Giardano to you yesterday."

"Schurf?" Jack didn't think Schurf would give the time of day to someone in the opposing camp.

Tiny turned to Schurf with a fake grin. "Let's just say that Mr. Schurf here has come around to our point of view."

Everyone looked at the obese attorney, who returned a weak, nervous smile.

Tiny stood and walked over behind Schurf's chair and looked down on the bald head. "Our new attorney here is now fully aware that Royster perjured himself in the Dranitzke case to shift all the blame away from himself and his FERK operation. Ed has been…," Tiny patted Schurf on the shoulder, "…persuaded to drop the Dranitzke suit against Dr. Giardano's estate, and assist us in taking appropriate action against Royster."

Jack's face dropped, his eyes moistened.

"What's wrong?" asked Tiny, returning to his chair.

Jack looked down at the table, then at Mrs. Giardano. "I don't have it. The disc, I mean. The hospital administrator has it."

"What?" Mrs. Giardano quavered.

"Today. This morning. I met with the Metrocare Hospital Administrator, Mr. Crantz. I wanted to get him to see the flimsiness of the data that's left. But he caved in completely. He invited Royster to the meeting and ended up siding with Royster's lies about the data. I had to hand the disc over to Crantz. And Royster had already confiscated the backup."

"Oh, no," cried Mrs. Giardano.

"Did Crantz give the original to Royster?" asked Tiny.

"No. Crantz still has it, in fact, has it right now at the Plaza. I saw it. We've got to do something. The first operation is tomorrow."

"Tomorrow?" Tiny and Mrs. Giardano chorused.

Jack nodded. "Live television coverage."

"We'll have to act tonight," Tiny said, "and Crantz is our man. He returns the disc to us, the hidden data is recovered, the authorities are contacted, tonight. That's it. Dr. Stegall, Crantz will cooperate, right?"

"I don't know. He might," Jack thought again. "But it could also backfire, badly, very badly. When I tell Crantz about the hidden data, he could just take the disc to his office, transfer the good data to another disc, and destroy the original. Royster could do the same thing to his copy. Those are the only two copies. All the evidence would be…"

"Finito," said the widow.

"Right," said Tiny. "Tutto e fineto. We've got to get that disc back, safe, intact, tonight."

Glancing at Schurf, Jack got an idea. "What about a subpoena? With Mrs. Giardano's story, wouldn't the courts produce a subpoena and issue a stop and desist…?"

Schurf, breaking his prolonged silence, spoke with a froggy throat. "You mean a restraint order. There isn't a chance. Not on such short notice. It would take weeks, maybe months."

"Maybe there's a way here," Jack said. "Crantz put the disc in his briefcase, and he has that briefcase with him right now at the Ball. If I could retrieve the disc, we would have the upper hand. Crantz would have no choice but to review the data and act accordingly."

Tiny and Mrs. Giardano exchanged glances, then she looked down with discouraged eyes.

Schurf whispered something into Tiny's ear, and Tiny nodded in agreement.

"Dr. Stegall," Tiny said, "you must return to the Plaza, obtain the disc, then inform this Crantz of its contents. If he refuses to cooperate, you immediately go to the higher ups."

"The hospital Board of Trustees and the FDA," Jack replied. "With pleasure."

"Good."

"And if I fail to get the disc?"

"Royster and Crantz still don't know about the hidden data. Then we resort to a subpoena and restraint of action order."

"And of course that could take a long time. And who knows if it will work?"

"It might not. But our best shot is tonight." Tiny wiped droplets of perspiration from his upper lip and loosened his tie.

So let's get moving," said Jack. "Mrs. Giardano, I need the the exact information about accessing the hidden data."

Mrs. Giardano removed a small business card from the envelope and slid it across the table to Jack. On the back, it read:

FERK DATA RECONSTRUCTION

1. Back out of dBASE
2. Go to Utility File "Filer"
3. To retrieve and merge removed data, cursor to "Myopia." Activate program.

What had seemed hopelessly elusive to Jack now appeared obvious. "Of course! Bob parked the data in a utility file called 'Filer'. Ingenious!"

"I'm not a computer person," Mrs. Giardano said, "but that sounds like what he told me. And he said that the whole thing would be restored with just…"

Jack eagerly finished her sentence. "Of course, just pressing a few keys. The whole thing is programmed already. Go to Filer, cursor to Myopia, and press 'Enter' to activate the program. It's simple."

"No, no," she said. "Bob said there was a trick at the end, there were not one but two keys to press. It's not written on the card."

"Which keys?" asked Jack, ballpoint ready.

She looked uncertain. "I—he showed me on the keyboard. You hold down the "Shift" key, and then he pressed key number 7."

"Shift and 7. Got it," said Jack, scribbling notes.

She grabbed Jack's wrist. "No, no, that's not all of it. He said something else. He said the key was—the housekey, yes, he said it was the housekey to unlock the whole program, all of the hidden data. Yes, that's it. The housekey would unlock everything."

"The housekey?" Jack said, puzzled.

"Housekey?" repeated Tiny, rubbing his chin. Then, in Italian, "Chiave della casa?"

Mrs. Giardano shrugged. "He said it would unlock everything. He said it even would show…" Her voice faded.

"Some other complication, right. Bob told me himself."

The woman nodded. "Yes, something very bad. But I don't know what."

Something a murdered nurse might have known, Jack thought. He clicked his ballpoint closed. "That's OK. 'Shift' and number 7 is all we need. 'Shift,' 7. The big 7." A smile formed. "Gentlemen, Mrs. Giardano, it looks like our good Dr. Royster has just rolled craps." He slipped the card into his wallet.

CHAPTER *Twenty-two*

Gabe watched as the song came to its brassy finale.

"…it's up to you, New York, New York!" As the singers scurried from the stage, Royster reappeared, patted Vorov and Nakamura on the back, and held up his hands for quiet.

"And now it's time to meet the special individual who will be our FERK patient tomorrow morning. Let's give her a nice welcome."

To a loud drum roll, spotlights expectantly swept the left side of the stage. When Maria walked out smiling and waving to crowd, Gabe gasped, "Maria!"

Gabe's Voice was obliterated by the applause and the orchestra's fanfare as Maria was escorted offstage by a squad of ushers.

The head waiter leaned over Gabe's shoulder. "There's a call for you." She followed him to the foyer"

"Can you talk?" It was Jack, calling from the limosine.

Gabe cupped her hand over the phone. "Yes. I'm in the foyer telephone room. Jack! Maria's going to have the operation! She replaced the Chinese girl."

"Is she there?"

"No! They whisked her off to Metrocare to spend the night! I couldn't do anything! She…!"

Jack interrupted. "Gabe, you've got to talk to her right away. I met with Giardano's widow. Bob told her everything. The data is on that disc after all, hidden. She told me exactly how to dig it out."

"Great! It's on Royster's disc too?"

"Yeah, but he doesn't know it."

"Omigod. Then you have to get…"

"The disc back from Crantz, then get Crantz to shut down this whole crazy operation tonight."

"What about Maria?"

"You call her right away, get her out of Metrocare. But first we have to lift the disc from Crantz. When I get there, I'll have you distract him so I can snatch it."

"Jack, I'm afraid it will be too late!" She leaned out from the phone stall to bring the ballroom entrance into view. "Jack, listen to me. From where I'm standing, I can see the greeting table inside the ballroom." She leaned out as far as she could. "Jack! I can see the briefcase, and the disc is still there, right there for the taking. Let me get it now."

"No, Gabe, too risky. We have to divert Crantz's attention."

"But it may be our last chance."

"OK. Listen. Move now, as soon as we hang up, and go get the disc. Then call me back at…" He looked at the telephone. The number had been scratched out. "Driver, what's the phone number on this?"

"Can't give it out, doc. Unlisted. Security thing."

Jack reached into his tuxedo jacket, pulled out his pocket phone, and pressed the "Power" button. It lit up, bleeped, then displayed, "Low Battery."

"Gabe, you can't call me back. I'll call you."

"Not good, Jack. Everyone's leaving and using the phones and…"

Simultaneously they both blurted out, "Crantz is leaving for the airport!"

Jack felt sweat trickle down his neck. "I have to reach him right now." He paused. "Listen carefully. I'm going to call Crantz in exactly four minutes. I'll tell him to check his briefcase to show him the disc is gone. When he confirms it, only then will I tell him about the hidden data. All right?"

"OK, I guess so."

"Then I'll tell him to call Mrs. Giardano and her brother. It may be a long night, but by morning Royster and FERK will be sunk."

"I'm going now, Jack. It'll look like I'm just picking up another button."

"Good. As soon as you have the disc, just leave the ballroom floor, go downstairs, call Maria, and tell her we're coming over to get her out of there. I'll pick you up at the 59th street entrance in twenty minutes."

CHAPTER *Twenty-three*

Gabe walked back through the foyer to the entrance to the ballroom. She paused, opened her purse in preparation to drop in the disc, then entered the ballroom, where she ran into a thick crowd of guests saying their goodbyes at the door.

"Excuse me, excuse me," she said as calmly as possible as she squeezed by. Finally clear of the throng, she slowly walked over to the greeting table. From where she was standing, Crantz was nowhere in sight.

She reached down into the briefcase, touched a FERK button, then slid her hand slowly up to the back pocket with the disc.

"May I help you, my pretty young lady?"

Gabe looked up, her face turning white. It was Crantz. His lids hung low from the booze, the clip-on tie dangled from his unbuttoned collar.

"Looks like you are the lucky recipient of our very last button. May I do the honors?" Crantz picked up the button and clumsily started to pin it on.

"No thank you," said Gabe, voice quavering. "It's for my friend."

"Very good," said Crantz, handing over the gold button. "Have a wonderful time."

"But I…"

"Yes?"

"I, uh, I need another button," she choked out, throat dry. "Could you go get me one?"

He gazed down into the briefcase and shook his head. "No, this is the last one. Here, take mine." He removed the button on his lapel and gave it to her. "Have a ball."

He snapped the briefcase closed, and just as he turned to leave, an usher approached. "Mr. Crantz, you have a phone call. Where would you like to take it?"

Crantz looked annoyed. "Dr. Royster has invited me to his table. Bring a cordless phone."

As Gabe watched incredulously, Crantz marched to Royster's table, carrying the aluminum briefcase. He greeted Royster with a pat on the back, acknowledged the other table guests, and sat down, placing the briefcase on the floor. The usher returned with the remote phone.

"Did you find out who it is?" Crantz asked the usher.

"A Dr. Stegall, sir."

"Dr. Stegall?"

Royster, who was in the middle of telling a joke, overheard. "Oh, our Dr. Stegall. Now what do you suppose our malcontent wants now?"

Crantz started to rise to talk privately away from the table, when Royster put his hand on the administrator's shoulder and pressed firmly downward. "Relax, Emmet. Better take the call here." Royster whispered something to the usher, and moments later the usher reappeared with a second cordless phone.

"Conference call, sir?" asked the usher as he handed the phone to Royster.

"Yes, conference call."

The usher programmed the phones, and, at Royster's signal, Crantz depressed the hold button. "Crantz here."

"Dr. Stegall here," said Jack from the limousine which had crawled only ten blocks through a traffic jam. "Mr. Crantz, this is a matter of utmost urgency. Are you free to talk?"

Royster lowered his phone and signaled an affirmative at Crantz. Crantz nervously looked over at Royster and nodded. Gabe, 50 feet away, helplessly watched as Royster dictated every word Crantz said.

Crantz pulled out a fresh handkerchief. "Yes, I can talk," he told Jack.

"Good," Jack said, relieved. "Mr. Crantz, I met Dr. Giardano's widow this evening. It's about the FERK research data. First, the computer disc I gave you has been returned to me."

Crantz looked perplexed. "What do you mean, returned to you? What are you talking about?"

"Check your briefcase. You'll see the disc is no longer there."

Crantz retrieved his briefcase off the floor and opened it. Both he and Royster could see the disc was safe and sound. Crantz looked catatonic.

Royster scribbled on a napkin. "Play along."

"What?" uttered Crantz, reading the words and turning to Royster in astonishment.

Royster returned Crantz an unyielding look.

Crantz wiped fresh beads of sweat from his forehead and spoke into the phone. "OK, Stegall, so the disc isn't there. What's going on here, what's this all about?"

Jack's heart leapt. Gabe had succeeded. The plan was working. "OK, Crantz," he said. "There's important data hidden in another file on the disc. I can't tell you all the details now, but essentially the FERK project is based upon data fraud."

"Fraud?"

"Yes. You must call Mrs. Robert Giardano immediately, and meet with us later tonight at Metrocare Hospital."

Crantz, his face as pale as the tablecloth, looked at Royster. "Dr. Royster," his lips trembled, "he says there's fraud. Dr. Royster, I…"

Royster reached in his breast pocket, removed the thick envelope the wealthy older woman had given him minutes before, and slid it directly in front of Crantz. "Emmet," he said softly. "This contains 50 thousand dollars given me tonight for stocks in our good cause. There's more where this came from, so, Emmet, I believe this should belong to you now. May I please have the disc from your briefcase, and then your telephone?"

Crantz looked at the sealed envelope, picked it up, felt its weight. Finally, he placed it in his own side pocket, turned, and extracted the disc. Royster gently lifted it from Crantz's fingers, then took the phone from his other hand.

He depressed the hold button. "Stegall, this is Royster."

At the sound of Royster's voice, Jack bolted upright in the limousine seat, dumbstruck.

"Stegall! You there?" Royster said into the silence on the other end of the line.

"Royster?" Jack uttered at last, hating the tremor in his voice.

"Yes. Stegall, I happened to overhear your malicious little plan to sabotage us. Let me set you straight. First, whatever scheme you had arranged to steal the disc has failed. I have the disc right here in my hand. Second, just in case you've slipped some phonied-up data onto these discs, rest assured that after we transfer the legitimate data to another disc we'll wipe the originals as clean as a whistle. That will eliminate any contaminations for good. Finally, you better prepare yourself for answering to administration on this, and, I might add, on your slandering FERK to medical students. Stegall, you're finished at Metrocare."

Jack felt he would explode. "Put Crantz back on," he yelled into the phone. "Do you hear me? Put him back on!"

Royster shouted, "Stegall, you're not in any position to tell anybody to do anything at this point!"

"You won't get away with this! You won't!"

Jack heard the click as Royster hung up. Only a shred of self-control prevented him from hurling the phone out of the vehicle's window. Wearily he let it drop to the floor. Everything had gone wrong. The only thing left was the subpoena Schurf had mentioned, and even that would take weeks, long after Royster had erased both discs. The only thing to do was to get Gabe's roommate out of Metrocare.

"Plaza," he barked at the driver.

The driver gave a thumbs up, only to slam on the brakes as the limo plunged into swarm of traffic.

Jack glanced out the window at the corner newspaper stand, and saw the bold headline on the New York Enquirer, "Murdered Woman Identified."

"Wait!" Jack dashed from the car, bought a copy, and flipped the page to the story. It read, "The woman stabbed to death on Friday at Metrocare Hospital was Pamela Wilcox, a 35-year-old Registered Nurse from Jersey City, New Jersey. Police stated that her identity was traced using her contact lens prescription and her affiliation with the Hudson County Nurses Association. Co-workers at the Jersey City General Eye Ward reported she had been missing for several days..."

Jack leapt back into the limosine. "Get to the Plaza as fast as you can!"

CHAPTER *Twenty-four*

Gabe watched Royster drop the disc in his briefcase and snap it closed. She strode from the ballroom—with Ms. Gutkopf moving swiftly behind her—to the foyer telephones.

"This is an emergency," Gabe gasped, cutting to the front of the waiting line and grabbing the nearest telephone. She dialed Metrocare. The line was busy. She dialed again. Still busy. "Maria!" she cried. She slammed down the phone, and came tearing out into the foyer amidst dozens of guests making their departure. "Out of my way!" she cried. "Out of my way!"

Ms. Gutkopf quietly watched her departure. Then she moved away from the crowd, produced her own cellular phone, and dialed.

The dilapidated pay phone at the edge of Mercy Park rang and rang. Finally out of the shadows a figure appeared, lifted the receiver with a meaty hand, and answered with a gravelly voice.

"We've got a big problem," Ms. Gutkopf began.

Gabe flew down the grand staircase and raced out of the 5th Avenue entrance where she encountered a line of weary ball-goers waiting for cabs. She turned frantically to one of the parking valets. "Do you remember my escort's car, the silver Porsche?"

The valet nodded.

"Get it as fast as you can. Please hurry!" She grabbed a ten dollar bill from her purse and crushed it into his hand. In less than a minute came the squeal of tires around a corner, and Jack's car appeared. Gabe jumped in, shifted, and accelerated, shooting backwards before realizing she had the gearshift in reverse. She shifted into low, pulled out of the hotel into the street-lit darkness, and made the right onto 5th. She had gone no more than half a block when it started to rain.

No sooner had she switched on the wipers when the rain fell in sheets, transforming the cars and taxis ahead into a smeared pattern of weaving, streaking tail lights and blinking directional signals. Straining forward to see through the flooded windshield, she barely managed to make the right turn on 57th Street when out of nowhere a stalled truck appeared directly in her path. She slammed on the brakes and cut her wheels hard to the left, narrowly avoiding a collision.

She pushed onwards, cursing beneath her breath and squinting against the splintering headlight beams from oncoming vehicles until she reached Broadway where the rain and traffic finally eased. Picking up speed, she at last made the turn south on 9th Avenue, and moments later pulled into the doctors' garage entrance opposite Metrocare Hospital.

She fumbled in the side pockets of the door, found Jack's parking card to activate the gate, drove in, and took the first available space. She jumped from the car and started for the elevator to Ninth Avenue. As she waited for the elevator to rise, a footfall made her turn.

A hand reached out from behind and clamped across her mouth. A strong forearm followed, yanking her backwards by the waist. She immediately tried to break free, but the grip on her body was overpowering, and she felt herself hauled toward an adjacent stairwell. She lost one high heel, then the other, and finally found herself stumbling down a flight of steps. When she looked up, and her eyes stopped at the level of her attacker's belt: the buckle read, "Don't Be Cruel." She looked higher, saw the filthy rain coat, the muscular body, the bald head, the missing teeth, the black patch. It was Bird.

"What are you doing? I'm—I'm a medical student!" she blurted as she struggled to her feet. Bird pushed her down again, reached under his rain coat, and pulled out a long object through his belt. It was the cane, the same cane that had been used to beat Quimby in the park.

"Shutup." Bird reached to the inside of his left boot and pulled a Smith and Wesson snub-nosed .357 Magnum revolver. He flipped it from one hand to the other, the gun's blue metal wet and glinting in the dim light.

Suddenly steps tapped toward them from one landing above. Bird turned towards the sounds. With Bird diverted Gabe crouched, then uncoiled with three successive reverse karate punches, the first to his throat, the second to his mouth, the last to his forehead. He fell back stunned. She started to run down the stairs but Bird caught the hem of her dress and rose up behind her with an arm-lock around the neck. Gabe's face began to redden and bulge with the blood trapped in the neck veins. Finally, with one enormous effort, she hurled Bird over her shoulder with a perfectly executed Judo throw, and he pitched face down on the landing. When he lifted his head, the eyepatch was gone, revealing a black, excavated socket. He grasped the cane, and just as Gabe raced by, struck her squarely in the forehead. The force of the swing caused him to lose his balance, and he fell headlong down the steps and smashed into a wall, unconscious.

Gabe stumbled toward the hospital, making her way into the ER where she collapsed on the floor. Moments later she was lying in the first trauma bay where a swarm of doctors and nurses immediately went to work and started an IV. As two female orderlies wiped her body with a sponge, two doctors scanned her body for penetrating wounds.

"What's your name?" demanded the nurse in charge.

Gabe was barely able to reply. "Richards," she managed. "Gabe. Med 4."

"My God! She's a medical student!" Hastily the nurse applied a blood pressure cuff. "Get Dr. Baker, stat."

Seconds later he was in the bay. "Gabe. Can you understand me?" he said close to her ear. "You've taken a bad blow to the head. Do you know if you were struck anywhere else, or shot?"

Gabe responded with a slow motion of her head "no."

"She's slipping in and out of consciousness," Baker stated. He checked her reflexes, and reinspected the swelling above her brow. "I want a CT scan stat, and I want neurosurgery here. Stat! Stat!"

The nurses scattered, while an intern and an orderly wheeled Gabe from the bay down the corridor towards the CT scan department.

Moments later Jack tore to the room and almost collided with Dr. Baker who was coming through the doorway with an orderly and nurse.

"Jack!" Baker said. "I guess you know. Your medical student in there, Gabe, has a closed head injury. Hold it for a second." He turned to the nurse and handed her a small wallet-sized card. "Here, it was in her purse. Try calling her insurance company. Best way to track down her parents fast."

"What happened?" asked Jack, starting to go around Dr. Baker to enter the room.

"Calm down, Jack, she…"

Jack tried to go around him again, and Baker had to grab his sleeve to restrain him. "Jack, calm down. Let me fill you in before you go in there. She was attacked in the parking garage. She suffered a blow to the right frontal area above the brow. She's got a mild TBI…"

"Traumatic brain injury. How bad?"

"Varies. Verbal and motor responses are up and down. On the Glasgow Coma scale, she's running between an 11 and 13. Heart and lungs stable. Neurosurgery is in there now, reviewing the CT scan to make their assessment."

"Neurosurgery?"

Dr. Baker studied him for a moment. "Jack, how long have you known Gabe. Are you…?"

"I've known—we're close. Pretty close."

Baker raised his eyebrows. "I see. OK, let's go in. Wait, first…," Baker grabbed a white lab coat hanging on the corridor wall, and motioned to

Jack to put it on. Except for the black bow tie, it disguised his tuxedo completely.

Jack and Baker entered and approached Gabe who lay on the stretcher. Two doctors were on the opposite side, their backs turned as they looked up at a full set of CT scans of the brain and eyes clipped on the X-ray display screens.

Barely noticing the doctors, Jack concentrated fully on Gabe's appearance. He was immediately relieved to discover that her only apparent head injury was the abraded, discolored swelling above the brow. What alarmed him was her state of consciousness. Her eyes were only half open, and she seemed only vaguely aware of people in the room. But breathing on her own, Jack observed, looking at the small plastic oral airway in her mouth. He glanced up at the IV bottle to check that it was dripping properly.

CHAPTER *Twenty-five*

"Dr. Stegall?" asked Dr. Arnsdorf, surprised at Jack's presence.

It was the first time Jack had seen the new resident. Somehow he hadn't pictured the thick glasses, the weak smile and chin.

"Hello, Stegall," said Fred Matthews with characterisitic indifference, looking back up at the CT scan to continue his conversation with the resident. His seersucker suit looked like the same he'd worn two days prior. "So, come on. Tell me what you think, Arnsdorf."

Arnsdorf, making a final inspection of Gabe's right eye with a hand-held ophthalmoscope, described his findings. "I think, um, severe trauma to the right superior orbital bony rim just beneath the brow. Vision, at least a few minutes ago when she was a little more responsive, was normal in the opposite eye, but she only could count my fingers with the right. The right pupil is relatively dilated and only constricts when I shine my flashlight in her left eye."

Jack interrupted. "Thanks, Dr. Arnsdorf, but I'll take over now. Gabe is my medical student, and I'll be in charge here."

Arnsdorf looked blankly at him, then at the other two doctors, and back at Jack. "I'm sorry, Dr. Stegall," he said, "but we've already con-tacted the on-call docs."

"Of course," Jack said, realizing he had totally disregarded hospital referral protocol. The doctor on call was always the responsible one. The transfer of responsibility to Jack would come after that. "Who's on call? I'll contact him. Is it Goldstein?"

Matthews, still reviewing the CT scan, gruffly answered over his shoulder. "It's Dr. Royster."

"Royster?" Jack blurted. "Royster can't be on this." He turned to Dr. Baker. "He's at a party, and anyway he doesn't know head trauma."

Ed Baker looked at all three doctors, then said, "Jack, Dr. Arnsdorf is correct. Meeting or not, Royster is on the On Call List for eye. We just telephoned him at the…"

"No meeting," interrupted Jack. "He's hosting a big mucketymuck ball at the Plaza."

"Nevertheless, Jack, Royster has been contacted and has already been brought in on the diagnostic loop here. He wants to get Arnsdorf's assessment. I suppose you can ask Royster to hand over the case once Arnsdorf calls him with his status report."

"Hold on," said Jack. "Obviously Gabe is in no condition to decide her care. But her parents are. You have to reach them first."

"Exactly what the nurse is doing now," replied Baker. "Jack, we don't object to your volunteering any advice here, but Royster is calling the shots for right now. When we reach her parents, they're free to choose any consultant they wish, including you."

A nurse walked in, and handed Baker a note. He read it and looked over at Jack. "When did Gabe talk to her parents last?"

"Monday night. Why?"

"Did you know they were going on a trip?"

"Yes, she said something about it."

"We called their home, and there's a message on their answering machine. Her whole family—father, mother and brother—are in Brazil, somewhere up the goddamn Amazon." He handed Jack the note.

"You can't be serious!"

"That's what it says. I'm sorry, but there's no way of getting in touch with them right now."

"What does that mean?"

Baker scratched his head. "Hospital regulations provide for this. In an emergency, the attending doctors are authorized to act on the patient's behalf, until the emergency has been resolved. If further intervention is required, administration is brought in, secondary consultation obtained."

"In other words," Matthews broke in impatiently, "it means we are right back where we were a half hour ago. We have a semi-comatose patient who is going blind in her right eye, and Royster and I are running the show."

Baker unhooked the ophthalmoscope and handed it to Jack. "Go ahead, Jack. I'm sure nobody here objects to your taking a look and commenting."

"Whatever," harrumphed Matthews, looking at his watch, "but can we get this show on the road? If this young lady needs my services, I don't want to spend all night talking about it. And Royster is waiting for us to call back."

Jack silently agreed. But as he looked at Gabe's face again, he noticed something that Arnsdorf hadn't mentioned: her right eye seemed to bulge forward slightly. The finding confirmed what Jack knew was the most likely diagnosis, and certainly the first working diagnosis of choice: Gabe had a small blood clot in front of the brain, which was interfering with the blood supply to the optic nerve. Rarely a blow on the forehead caused such a clot. It all fit. His tension began to ease. Thank goodness Gabe's brain was OK, he thought. If she needed anything, it was a simple procedure to relieve the pressure of the clot, and, as an eye surgeon, he would be the one to do it.

Arnsdorf walked up to the CT scan. "My diagnosis is compression of the optic nerve."

"What?" blurted Jack.

"Good, Arnsdorf," said Matthews. "That is exactly my diagnosis. Looks like our young lady here will go on our optic nerve compression protocol. We'll put her on steroids IV for 8 hours, and if her vision and pupil don't return to normal, we'll do a transfrontal unroofing of her optic canal." He flicked off the lights on the screen, and jabbed his pen into the pocket of his seersucker jacket.

"Wait a minute!" Jack snapped. "A brain operation? I disagree. You failed to notice that her right eye is bulging. The most likely diagnosis here is a blood clot behind the eye! There's no question about it!"

Dr. Matthews yanked a penlight from his pocket and flashed it at Gabe's eye as if to check Jack's finding. "I'll accept that there may be a little swelling of the eye," he sniffed, poking the penlight back in his shirt pocket, "but I see no evidence of a blood clot behind the eye." The brain surgeon shut his briefcase. "You agree Arnsdorf?"

Arnsdorf nodded nervously.

"Gentlemen, gentlemen," intervened Baker. "If I may. For my benefit, and for this patient's, what the hell are you people talking about?"

Jack turned to Baker with pleading eyes. "Arnsdorf is saying that the force of the blow to Gabe's right brow was transmitted through the skull to the canal through which the optic nerve passes from the brain to the eye."

Arnsdorf defensively broke in. "I'm saying, Dr. Baker, that the bone around the nerve may be fractured."

"And that even if it was fractured, it may not show up on CT scan," added Dr. Matthews.

"…and that means?" asked Baker impatiently.

"What they're saying," said Jack, glaring at Matthews, "is that her right optic nerve is being compressed."

"You mean like the median nerve in the wrist of a carpal tunnel syndrome?" asked Baker.

"Exactly," Jack replied. "And if they were correct, she would need an emergency brain operation to relieve the pressure."

"Otherwise the optic nerve will die, and the eye goes blind," said Dr. Matthews cockily.

"True," said Jack, the fingernail digging in. "But, Ed, I disagree with this diagnosis and treatment plan. It's possible, but the most likely diagnosis is that Gabe has a blood clot just behind the eye which can be relieved with a simple eye operation. That's why the eye is bulging slightly."

"Who would operate?" Baker asked.

"An eye surgeon. Me!"

Sensing the growing tension in the room, the nurse monitoring Gabe's blood pressure excused herself and vanished through the door.

"Now let's get back to basics, Stegall," Matthews said. "We appreciate your concern, but Royster is the ophthalmologist on call, and he's the one who is consulting on this case."

Jack flashed Dr. Baker a desperate look.

Baker shrugged. "Jack, I understand how strongly you disagree, but Royster is…"

The phone rang, and the nurse who had just walked back in picked it up. "It's Dr. Royster."

Baker looked at Arnsdorf. "OK, give him your report."

When the resident took the phone his hand trembled and his voice shook. "Yes, Dr. Royster. It's what we suspected at the first, optic nerve compression." For a moment he listened silently. Finally, "Yes sir, hold on." He handed the phone to Matthews.

Matthew's said, "Right. It's pretty clear cut. If the steroids don't work I'll go in surgically tomorrow morning. First case. Eight o'clock sharp. Oh, Stegall is here. He thinks there might be a hemorrhage behind the eyeball." There was a long pause. "No, CT scan shows nothing to definitely corroborate it." Another pause. "OK."

He hung up.

"What did he say?" asked Jack. "Does he see my point? When will he be here?"

"He's not coming. He agrees it's clear cut."

"What do you mean, not coming?" Jack couldn't believe it. Royster may hate his guts, but Royster was on call and still fully responsible for Gabe whom he didn't know at all.

Matthews buttoned his jacket. "Royster is signing off on Arnsdorf's opinion and I've got my consultation. Now if you don't mind, I have some orders to write, and I have to brief my neurosurgery resident."

"Not coming? That's outrageous," Jack barked. "You're making a big mistake. This could be malpractice!"

Matthews looked Jack up and down. "C'mon, you know better than that, Doctor Stegall. There are four doctors on this—I, Royster, Arnsdorf, and Baker, who concur on this plan of treatment. Regardless of the outcome, I don't think a fifth doctor rushing into the middle of things claiming there's a blood clot is going to get us sued."

Jack started for the telephone to call Royster. "He has to come. He will see."

Matthews folded his notes and stuffed them in his pocket. "Dr. Stegall, I don't know exactly what it is with you and Royster, but I do not think you and he are on the best of terms."

"What do mean by that? What did he say?" demanded Jack.

"Frankly, he said you were a troublemaker, and full of it. That's a quote. You asked." He clicked his doctor's bag closed, and started to leave the room, with Arnsdorf close behind.

Jack caught Matthews by the arm.

"Get your hands off me!" Matthews tried to wrench his arm away, but Jack's grip was too strong. It took both Arnsdorf and Baker to drag Jack off the short brain surgeon.

"Don't touch me," Jack said to Arnsdorf, ripping the resident's hands away. To Baker he panted, "I'm OK." Only then did Baker release his grip.

Breathless and heart pounding, Jack glared at Matthews and Arnsdorf, who quickly moved towards the door. Arndsdorf turned and left the room, but Matthews stopped and glared at Baker. "This is my case, Ed. My first order is that I do not want Stegall around my patient. I want him outta here!" Matthews stormed out.

For a full minute the only sound in the room was the beep of Gabe's vital signs monitor and the sound of Jack's heavy breathing. Finally Baker spoke. "Please come with me to my office, would you Jack?"

"Wait." Jack went to Gabe for one last look. He felt her pulse, checked the IV, then gently lifted the upper lid of her right eye. At first it seemed just as before—pupil relatively mid-dilated, no other abnormality, until he noticed something unusual on the white part of the eye: a number of tiny red hemorrhagic dots, at least twenty. Petechial hemmorhages, thought Jack. Everyone had either missed them, or they were only now becoming visible. He looked up at Baker, and decided to say nothing. Jack had no definite clue why there would be petechial hemorrhages. It would be futile discussing the finding. He gently stroked back some wisps of Gabe's hair, turned, and followed Baker out of the room.

In Baker's cramped, chart-strewn office, Jack at first listened impassively. "I know how upset you are," Baker told him, "but I think everything will turn out OK. Gabe is going to be on medication through the night. Maybe she'll improve and Matthews won't have to operate at all."

At that, Jack found his voice with a vengeance. "Steroids won't work fast or far enough to stop Dr. Matthews from operating. The first thing that should be tried is an orbital incision to explore for a hematoma, or at least a simple tapping of the hematoma with a needle. Optic canal compression is extremely unlikely here. Surgery for it should be undertaken only as a last resort…"

Jack stopped short. Directly in front of him on the desk lay the Emergency Room On Call Schedule where Baker had tossed it. It was opened to the last page where the Neurosurgery Section had been encircled in pencil by Dr. Baker. To Jack's astonishment, there were three neurosurgeons listed on call, and Matthews was the third in line.

"What the hell?" Jack said, pointing to the names. "Ed, Matthews is third on call. Have you called the first two?"

Baker looked away and shook his head slowly. "You had to see that, didn't you?"

Jack took the list from the ring binder and thrust it in front of Baker's face. "Ed, what is this?"

Baker took the list and folded it in half. "Jack, would you please sit down and settle?"

Jack stood his ground. "I demand to know why one of the first two brain surgeons wasn't called in instead of that surgical wacko Matthews!"

"You're not going to like what you hear."

"Tell me."

"First you've got to sit down."

Jack sat down on the edge of a chair, looking ready to spring.

"You promise not to blow up, Jack?"

"Yes."

"Gabe's health insurance is a new managed care plan called Empire State Health Extra. It's the cheap one medical students get. We called the other two neurosurgeons on call first. Neither is on the plan, and a patient can't go out of the plan. Matthews, however, is on the plan. Christ, I think he's the only one on the face of the earth who is. Jack, we have no other choice but Matthews." Baker took a step back as if expecting Jack to explode, which he did.

"Have no choice?" Jack stood up. "Then at least replace Royster with someone on the plan!"

"I'm afraid that would be impossible, Jack."

"Why?"

"Jack, Royster is not only on the plan, he is the plan. I mean, he and one of his corporations formed that HMO three years ago and have been raking it in every since."

"Royster formed the plan? Why would he let someone like Matthews on the plan? They know he's a huge risk!"

"Jack, you are not going to like the answer."

"What is it?"

"Matthews did big-time what Royster asked all of the HMO docs to do."

"Which was?"

Baker looked down at his desk and shook his head. "Matthews put every dime he had into Globe stocks."

"Matthews is a stockholder?"

Baker threw his hands in the air. "Jack, I didn't do this! Calm down!"

Jack grabbed the list from Baker's hand, crumpled it in his fist, and hurled it across the room. "Ed, you've got to listen to me! This whole disaster is because of Royster. He just calls in from his big shindig at the Plaza, carelessly accepts Dr. Arnsdorf's diagnosis, and his HMO buddy Matthews gets his go-ahead to operate." Jack slammed his fist on the desk. "You have to do something! You've heard the rumors about Matthews! In the operating room, he's an accident waiting to happen!"

Baker opened his mouth but words failed him.

"Ed, you have to stop this!" Jack started to pace.

"I can't," insisted Baker. "Look, you're real upset. I know what you must be going through. Giardano's death was a terrible shock. Look, there's absolutely nothing I can do and nothing you can do. I'm sorry. You just have to hope for the best."

"You really mean that? That's it?"

"That's it, unless Gabe comes out of her stupor or the medicines take effect and…"

"She won't improve in the next 8 hours. You can't let her head be cracked by that surgical speedfreak!"

"Jack, leave it alone for now." Baker went to the door to make sure it was closed. "Listen, Jack, Royster said something else on the phone. It has to do with some big TV operation scheduled for tomorrow. He told me that you'd been meddling in the whole thing. He told me to tell you not to contact the patient about the operation, to meddle no further. Not to contact…," he pulled out a slip of paper from his white coat pocket, "…this Maria S. woman."

"Sanchez. Maria Sanchez."

"So you do know about her."

"Yes I do. She's Gabe's roommate. That's why Gabe raced over here tonight, to meet me and then…," Jack stopped.

"And then what?"

"To, you know, talk to Maria to wish her good luck. They're real good friends." Jack couldn't look Baker in the eye for fear he would see the deception. "Maria is nervous about it and can use some support. Royster is so uptight about this show going right, I guess he's become a little paranoid. Anyway, there's no problem now. Gabe is my concern now, not her roommate."

Baker looked at Jack appraisingly. "Maybe so. But I have my responsibilities. I'm going to have heavy security posted at the entrance of the OR tomorrow morning checking everybody's I.D.. Don't think of showing up, Jack, because you'll just be denied entrance. You can check on Gabe and her friend tomorrow, but stay away from that OR, understand?"

Jack barely nodded.

"Good. Now, Jack, you look like you've had it. Go home and get some rest."

"No, thanks."

Baker's eyes grew more serious than ever. "Jack, can I give you some unsolicited advice? Tonight you were about to duke it out with another doctor. Man, I'm not saying I haven't felt the same way a thousand times, but you are crossing the line bigtime. There are higher-ups around here that just love to go after people who cross the line, Jack. Be careful. Think of your goddamned career. Once you fall off the tightrope, they don't let you get back up. Let it go, Jack. Go home, get some rest, and check on your friends tomorrow. And stay away from that OR."

"I guess you're right, Ed," Jack replied, wondering if his handball partner could detect the false tone in his voice. They shook hands. "I'll be back tomorrow to check on Gabe. I know you've done everything you can." The men said goodbye, and Jack left the office.

Jack walked out of the emergency room. Ignoring a cold rain that had begun, he crossed the roadway and entered the darkness of Mercy Park. The police had completed their investigation and cleared out completely, a few scraps of yellow NYPD crime scene tape their only remaining traces. By the time he reached the park's central circle, his white lab coat was half-soaked, and his hair hung in rivulets on his forehead and neck. He paused to circle the statue. His search stopped when he discovered Quimby sitting on the stone ledge on the opposite side of the statue, gazing blankly at the ground. Somehow he'd found an old poncho and stocking cap to wear over his sopping wet clothing.

"Quimby. There you are." Jack sat next to him.

"How is she doc?" asked Quimby.

"You saw what happened?"

"Yeah, man. I was in the parking garage."

"Tell me exactly what happened."

Quimby shivered beneath his poncho. "She fought him. You know, with that ju jitsu Chinese fight stuff. She gave him a good fight. She flipped him over and broke the choke hold."

"Choke hold! So that's what made the blood vessel break behind the eye." Jack went over it in his mind. The chokehold and the throw must have caused an acute venous blood pressure rise in Gabe's head. The pressure was transmitted to a vein behind the right eye, and the vein must have ruptured, causing the hematoma. But tiny veins in the front ruptured also. That explained the dots, the petechia. The blow to the forehead with the cane had only caused a concussion. Now Jack knew he was right. He thanked Quimby and got up to leave.

"Wait a minute, doc," said Quimby. He fumbled beneath his poncho and pulled out a soaked teeshirt. "This was Bird's. See?"

In the dim light Jack could make out the lettering. "Globe, Inc. Then Bird was working for them?"

Quimby nodded.

"He was the one behind your getting beat up, wasn't he?"

Quimby nodded again. "I couldn't say nothin' till now, ya understan' what I'm sayin'?"

"Thanks, Quimby." Jack turned to go.

And he made a point to take the heavy cane with him.

CHAPTER *Twenty-six*

THURSDAY

As Jack predicted, at 7:15 a.m. nobody would be in the Hospital Laundry Department located in the far reaches of the hospital basement except for one night shift employee.

"Can I help you?" the elderly attendant said, looking up from a small TV set.

"I'm here from the OR." Jack said. "We're giving a little surprise party for one of the doctors, and I'm supposed to show up as an orderly. You have plenty of size large scrubs, don't you?"

At first the attendant hesitated, but then looked back through bifocals at the TV. "The supply lady can help you. She'll be here in…"

"I can just grab them. Where's the bathroom?"

"In the back." The attendant fiddled with the TV controls.

Jack walked into the supply room. Dozens of racks held sheets, blankets, pajamas, and OR garb. Jack found a set of large orderly scrubs, and disappeared into the bathroom. He quickly changed, and came outside. "Caps and masks?" he asked the attendant.

"By the wall behind you," the man answered, still watching his TV set.

"Good program?"

"Yeah, you know, they're going to show that fancy new eye operation on TV this morning. It's a big deal. Should come on any minute."

"Great." Jack put on the largest surgical hood he could find. Then he loosely tied on a mask so as to half cover his mouth.

"Thanks a lot," he said.

"Happy party."

Outside housekeeping, Jack immediately saw what he was looking for—a tall rack on wheels loaded to the top with surgical scrubs. Nobody was around. His luck was holding up, he thought, as he quietly began to roll the rack along the hall to the elevator. Again he checked the time: 7:40. He decided to give himself two more minutes.

His watch showed 7:42. It was time. He pressed the button for the elevator. When the doors opened, it was empty. He rolled the rack to the side of the elevator and stood behind it. Then he pressed the button for the 7th floor, the OR.

On the 1st floor, a dozen people jammed onto the elevator's remaining space. Jack recognized two medical students from Gabe's group, but, as he expected, they ignored a housekeeping orderly completely.

On the 3rd floor, a tall, blue-uniformed security guard boarded, walkie-talkie crackling. Jack kept his gaze to the ground, certain that at any moment everyone would hear his heart pounding and see the perspiration soaking through his scrub shirt. An eternity seemed to pass before the guard got off on the 4th floor, looked left and right while reporting into his walkie-talkie, then disappeared from view.

The elevator ascended to the 5th, where it half emptied. With Jack, two medical students, and a lab technician remaining, it finally glided towards seven. Jack braced, expecting that there, just outside the elevators, security would have its crucial checkpoint. If they asked him anything, he would just have to play dumb and fake an answer.

The doors opened. To his surprise there was only one guard, standing 10 yards down the corridor to the right towards the main entrance into the operating room. Better yet, security had totally overlooked the housekeeping entrance to the left.

After the students and the orderly stepped off and turned, Jack shouldered the heavy cart off and steered left. The guard seemed to take a vague interest in the students, but ignored Jack completely. At a deliberate slow pace, he reached the back entrance marked "O.R.—Do Not Enter.", and pushed the cart through the scuffed double doors.

Once inside, he went straight for the male surgeons' locker room. There he entered and went straight to his locker. He opened it, and retrieved the object he had placed there the night before—the wooden cane he would very much need in minutes.

He returned to the corridor and the laundry rack, where he buried the cane beneath a pile of fresh scrubs. Looking further down the hall, he saw exactly what he had planned for—one of the portable X-ray machines, a heavier model made by GE, standing unattended against the wall.

He pushed the rack another 20 feet, extracted the cane, then walked as calmly as possible to the X-ray machine. He unlocked its wheels, slid the cane into a side rack, and wheeled the cumbersome device forward.

As he'd expected he was ignored by the few OR personnel already scurrying about the back surgical passageways and soon he was at the intersection leading to the main corridor. Crossing it, he had a clear view of the preoperative staging area with dozens of gurneys bearing their cargo of patients scheduled for the 8:00 a.m. surgeries. Gabe was not in view, but it was obvious which stretcher contained Maria—the one surrounded by people.

Jack recognized most of them. Royster was in surgical scrubs, adjusting his OR cap while talking assuringly with Maria. Vorov and Nakamura, standing behind Royster, were drawing some kind of diagram on a clipboard, while Crantz and Craig jawed over some final detail. Arnsdorf was checking Maria's chart while a nurse took her blood pressure. Meanwhile a hospital photographer steadily circled the group, camera flashing.

Jack took one last look and finally caught a glimpse of Gabe at the other end of the staging area, attended by a single nurse going through the pre-operative checklist. Obviously Maria and Gabe were unaware of each other's presence. Jack had expected that. Even if Gabe had been fully conscious, the pre-operative staging area was expansive, and Maria and Gabe were at opposite ends. And surgery patients were always too preoccupied with their own fears to look around and find out who was in the same boat.

Instead of taking the usual route to the OR suites' main entrance, Jack turned along a narrow passageway to an auxiliary entrance from the rear. Pushing the heavy machine through the doors, he moved onwards, ignored by the nurses and orderlies making the final preparations for the 8:00 o'clock start. Finally, he turned the corner, and reached Suite 10, the neurosurgery suite.

After parking the machine just outside the door to the suite, he moved to the adjacent scrub basin alcove. Now, from his neutral corner next to the wall phone, he was in perfect strategic position. He could see down the corridor to the double doors through which they would bring Gabe. And he could view into the neurosurgery suite where they would wheel her. Already he could see the neurosurgical instrument nurse rolling instrument tables into position, while the circulating nurse laid out the cord for the craniotomy saw and began unwrapping sterile supplies required for brain surgery. The circulator turned, and Jack smiled inwardly. It was Cissy Brown. That's one for my team, he thought.

Jack looked up. The clock on the wall showed Five minutes to 8:00. 5 minutes, Jack thought, until the first round of patients were wheeled through. And among them would be Maria and Gabe.

Jack picked up the wallphone, pressed zero, and redirected his gaze back to the double doors. "Give me the control room of the Surgical Conference Theatre, please," Jack told the hospital operator.

After 6 rings the phone picked up. It was Charlie, the communications-computer engineer.

"Charlie, this is Stegall." Jack spoke barely above a whisper.

"Yeah, Jack, what's up?"

As Jack had calculated, the hospital hadn't alerted the control room about his escape. "How ya doing, Charlie? All set for the extravaganza?"

In the control room sitting before the main panel of TV monitors, Charlie switched to his headset. "Yeah, doc, this place looks like we're broadcasting the Superbowl. The theater is standing room only. You want reporters, trustees, bigwigs from Columbia, we got 'em. I expect the Fuji blimp to fly over any moment. Hold it for a second, Jack." Charlie handed a sheet of last-minute instructions to Markowitz, the director, sitting closeby in the main control chair, headset on, issuing final orders to the television crew. "We're going live with the Good Morning, USA show in just a few minutes," Charlie added. "What's up, Dr. Stegall?"

"Royster is getting ready to operate, and wanted me to give you a message. Charlie, you know the data disc that he's going to sequence during the countdown?"

"Yeah, it's all set to roll and scroll."

"And they're still going to have it narrated?"

"Right. Narrator's ready to go in the sound booth."

"Good. Listen, Charlie. In honor of Dr. Giardano, Royster wants to publicize all of the data, to include the stuff that Dr. Giardano worked especially hard on."

"Fine, Jack, but we're only about 5 minutes to air," Charlie said, fiddling with the color console. "What does this involve?"

"Simple. All you have to do is pick it up off of another file on the disc and merge it with what you have already."

"No problem, doc. What do I do?"

"Giardano made it real simple. The program is under a special file called 'Filer.' What program are you in now?"

"I'm in dBase."

"You have to back out of dBase first. Hit 'Escape' twice."

Charlie punched in the keystrokes. "OK, Jack. I just backed out. What now?"

"Now, just type the letter "f" and press 'Enter.'"

"I did it. Yeah, I see, I just got this list on the screen. I had no idea this file was in here. Pretty slick. What now?"

"OK, Charlie, now scroll down. You should see a file named 'Myopia.'"

Charlie pressed the down arrow. "Yep, there it is, 'Myopia.'"

"Good. That's the program which will retrieve the rest of the data and merge it with the previous data. Let's activate it."

"How?"

"Hold down the 'Shift' key, and press number 7."

Suddenly two network engineers descended on Charlie with a last minute question. Jack could hear Charlie setting the engineers straight. The few seconds felt like hours.

Charlie came back on. "Now, what was that again, Jack?"

"Hold down the 'Shift' key, and press number 7."

Charlie pressed the keys.

Nothing happened—the screen remained unchanged, the cursor flashing monotonously at the word 'Myopia.'

"Doc, sorry, no dice," said Charlie.

"What?" Jack exclaimed.

"I pressed your keys, but nothing changed. You sure you got your program correct?"

"Absolutely," Jack insisted. "Try it again, Charlie. Re-cursor to Myopia, hold 'Shift,' hit 7."

Charlie repeated the maneuver. "Sorry, doc. Not a thing."

Jack was stunned.

"You there, doc?" asked Charlie. "Doc, you there?"

Jack leaned up against the alcove wall. "Yes, I'm here," he answered, dejected, his voice gone husky. Somehow the program to merge the data was a failure. Where had Giardano gone wrong? There was no way of telling. He felt weak in the legs. Now his only course was to warn Maria directly. But with no proof, that seemed doomed to fail.

Charlie looked up at one of the control room wallclocks. 7:59. "About out of time, doc. Better forget it, whaddya say?"

"No, no. I'll call back. Can you just leave that screen on, leave the cursor on 'Myopia?'"

"Well, OK. Better make it fast, doc. We're just a few minutes to air."

"Is your headset on?"

"Yeah."

"Back in a minute." Jack hung up. He withdrew his list from his pocket and drew a question mark above the word "merge." The next line on the list read "Suite 10: Secure."

Jack looked at the corridor clock. It read 8:00 o'clock to the second. The double doors opened, and two gurney stretchers were pushed through. One carried an obviously ill, elderly patient, the other a huge man, his feet dangling over the edge of the stretcher. Jack pretended to be talking on the telephone as the stretchers were wheeled past him and the X-ray machine.

The doors opened again. Another pair of stretchers, one with a pediatric case, the other with the suspensory contraptions and casts of orthopedics.

The doors shut, then re-opened immediately. Backing through them was a battery-belted cameraman training his video steadicamera onto a wheelchair being pushed behind him, on which sat Maria, bright-eyed and wide-smiled. She was dressed in white silk evening pajamas and a light blue hospital terry cloth bathrobe. Her tied-up black hair was barely visible beneath a paper OR bonnet. Behind her walked Royster, pushing the wheelchair, and to his side Nakamura, Vorov, and two nurses.

As the entourage neared, Jack turned his face away, grabbed a clipboard hanging on the wall, and with the phone cradled between his shoulder and his ear began scribbling nonsense on the page. Without noticing him, the group passed by, the nurses giggling over the excitement of the event, and proceeded down the corridor towards Suite 13, the main eye suite.

Jack looked back at the doors. They were motionless. He looked at the clock. It was 4 minutes past eight. Craig's punctual OR schedule was rarely delayed that much. Could it be, he thought, that Gabe had improved and the craniotomy had been canceled? And was it possible that, even now, Jack could get through to the TV director and convince him to pre-screen the disc and cancel the show? Jack would still have to take his punishment for the attempted kidnapping of Gabe from the hospital, but—the disastrous consequences of what he was about to commit loomed in his imagination. Leniency would be out of the question. They would throw the book at him, kick him off the staff, report him to the State Medical Board. They would strip him of his license, he would be blackballed in every hospital, every medical society, every state in the country. He would be finished.

He reached for the phone to call the OR desk, desperate to hear that Gabe's operation had been cancelled. He hadn't touched the receiver when the double doors opened. There was no mistaking the runty profile of Dr. Matthews, walking alongside Gabe's stretcher as the orderly guided it towards the door to Suite 10. The operation was clearly going forward, and for Jack, there was no going back.

CHAPTER *Twenty-seven*

Gabe lay with an IV threaded into her arm. But she was still breathing on her own, a good sign. An oxygen mask covered the lower half of her face. Behind the stretcher walked Dr. Sam Bankert, reviewing Gabe's chart. Good, thought Jack. Bankert on the case meant he wouldn't go it alone.

With the orderly leading, they bumped through the door to the suite, rolled the stretcher in alongside the OR table, and lifted Gabe onto it. Cissy secured the arms, Bankert placed EKG leads, and Matthews positioned the head. When the scrub nurse finally slipped off the blue paper bonnet, the tresses of Gabe's dark wavy hair billowed forth, fell, and swayed above the vinyl floor.

Jack watched and waited. Dr. Bankert rolled the general anesthesia cart into position, then rechecked Gabe's IV. Dr. Matthews snapped the CT scan films on the viewer, and rechecked Gabe's pupils. He nodded at the scrub nurse—a signal to shave Gabe's hair—then walked through the side door into the same scrub basin alcove Jack was standing in. Standing no more than six feet from Jack, the brain surgeon leaned over the basin and began to soap. The moment had arrived. "Showtime," Jack whispered softly.

Jack walked out into the corridor, unlocked the X-ray machine, and rolled it into the suite. "X-ray," he said. Nobody looked over. Jack immediately pushed the machine over to the side door, flush against it. He relocked the wheels, grabbed some heavy Velcro straps from an adjacent cabinet, and lashed the machine to the door handle. The door from the the scrub alcove was now safely anchored closed by the 600 pound load.

Jack walked over to the scrub nurse, who had just turned on the electric razor. "Got a message," Jack said. "You're wanted down the hall to pick up another craniotomy saw." She turned off the razor, set it aside, and left the suite. Close on her heels was the orderly, wheeling out the empty guerney.

That left Jack, Bankert, and Cissy in the room.

As soon as the guerney had cleared the door, Jack went to the X-ray machine and fetched the cane. Returning to the door, he wedged one end of the cane under the door handle, the other end beneath a steel bracket on the wall next to the jam. He tried the door. Shut like a rock. The heavy staff was working perfectly as a huge dead bolt.

He looked through the side window to the alcove. Matthews was still scrubbing, entirely oblivious to the action inside the suite. Jack walked over to Dr. Bankert who was listening to Gabe's chest. Jack tapped him on the shoulder.

The anesthesiologist looked up, and recognized him immediately. "Stegall. What the…?"

Jack held his index finger up to his masked mouth in a gesture warning silence.

Cissy looked up. "Dr. Stegall!" she stammered.

Jack, his voice low and insistent, enunciated each syllable. "Sam, Cissy, I have to talk to you right now. Do you think we've been friends long enough for you to listen to me?"

Sam and Cissy looked at each other, then nodded in agreement. Sam noticed the X-ray machine blocking the side door, the cane bolting the main door. He looked at Gabe's draped body, then back at Jack. "This better be real good, Jack. I don't think what I see unfolding here strictly complies with operating room procedures."

Through the window separating the suite from the scrub alcove, Jack could see Matthews rinsing his arms and hands.

"Here's the deal," Jack said. "The patient is Gabe Richards, Sam. She's the student you and I worked with on Monday."

"I know, Jack. I just now learned."

"Last night she was struck in the forehead. She's neurologically intact with a negative CT scan, except she has the mid-dilated pupil on that side. Royster was on call, never saw her, and signed off on the resident's diagnosis, which was optic nerve compression in the canal. They refuse to understand that Gabe has a retrobulbar hematoma which could be the whole problem. Matthews is charging ahead with brain surgery. But she just has a clot in front."

"Used to see it in Nam all the time," said Bankert. "But why don't they listen to you?"

"No time to explain. Sam, will you sedate her long enough for me to try an evacuation?"

Suddenly the side door shook to a heavy pounding. Everyone looked over to see Dr. Matthews banging on the thick glass of the obstructed door with his unscrubbed elbows. "Get the damned machine out of the way," he snarled.

"Jesus," Bankert said. "Jack, is this the only way?"

"Believe it or not, Sam, it's the only way, and it's going to get worse."

Bankert and Cissy exchanged looks of fright. The racket grew louder.

"Sam," Jack said. "Maybe you shouldn't. Wouldn't want to get Craig upset, right?"

"You charmer," said Bankert. "OK, here we go. Let's get moving before Fast Fred tears the door down." He cracked open an ampule of Deprivan. "How about you Cissy? You in?"

At Matthews' pounding, Cissy had brought her hands to her ears. "Dr. Stegall, Dr. Bankert may be retiring, but I'm not. Look, I'll help you gown, but I better stay out of any unauthorized operation."

"OK. Just the gown," said Jack. He saw the terror in her eyes.

The loud banging now echoed from the front door, where Matthews had run to find that route blocked as well. Behind him stood the ejected scrub nurse, utterly mystified. Jack turned, and through the glass Matthews recognized him. "Stegall!" he shouted, beating even harder. "Stegall! What the hell are you doing! Get the hell out of there! Let me in!"

Dr. Matthews gave one final slam on the window with both fists. "I'll be back with Craig and the police." Eyes popping with rage, he disappeared down the corridor in the direction of the head nurse's office. The scrub nurse backed away to the opposite wall and continued to look on in disbelief.

Drawing up the Deprivan in a syringe, Bankert threw Jack a doubtful glance. "Jack, how long do you think it's going to be before Craig gets engineering to chainsaw their way in here?"

"Sam, I only need 10 minutes, 15 max."

"What's the rush?"

"There's another operation to stop."

"Who?"

"Maria Sanchez."

"Jack, do you mind my asking just how many patients you've got up here today?" asked Bankert as he and Cissy attached the Ohmeda automatic sphygmomanometer and Okidata pulse oximeter,

"Maria's Gabe's roommate." Jack quickly rechecked Gabe's right eye, then sat down at the MegaMOM console and scanned the key template.

Bankert looked up at the monitor displaying the surgical schedule. "Sanchez. That's Royster's big laser show. Why the extra heroics?"

"Comes with the territory, Sam." Jack logged onto the computer. "I've got to reprogram MegaMOM right away, starting with override. What's the code?"

Sam's eyebrows raised. "Woah. Override? Heavy duty, Jack. You sure?"

"Positive."

"Just enter the word 'override' spelled backwards and hit 'Escape'."

Jack keyed it in.

Seconds later, the screen displayed a layout of the OR's entire audio-visual system. Then a question appeared. "Do you wish total remote AV control?"

Jack keyed in affirmative.

Then "Type your name and AV special I.D. number."

Jack complied.

Moments later, "You now have total remote control of AV system. Indicate location."

Jack typed in "Suite 10."

After a pause, the computer blinked the message: "Master remote control, Suite 10, operational."

Jack wiped beads of perspiration from his forehead. It had taken him fully a minute to key in the network he'd planned. Now he could send or receive audio and video signals from every site in the operating room to his suite and back. He was in total remote override.

He keyed in for the main eye suite, and looked up at the video monitors. Maria, now clad only in the silk white pajamas, had already been transferred from the wheelchair to the seat on the Myogoround. Vorov stood beside her, ready to activate the "On" button. Inside the suite, Royster was in firing position at the FERK machine's free-electron beam emitter, while Nakamura manned the control panels to the side. All three were in their scrubs, masks, and headsets. In a corner window of the second monitor, Jack saw the shot of the observation chamber above, with Craig, Crantz, Gutkopf and several medical students staring down into the suite.

Jack donned his own headset, and keyed into the SCT control room. Now he could audit the entire progress of the show. He looked up at the clock: 8:11. Suddenly he heard the director's voice.

"Beautiful, beautiful. Everything, everyone looks great. We are about to begin. We are about ready to go live with the Good Morning, USA show. Break a leg, everybody." The director paused to receive last minute instructions from the coordinator at the main television studio.

"OK, doctors, crew, everybody, we are just about to be introduced on the show. I'm going to switch your monitors to what they're airing."

The image on the "Air" video monitors flickered and switched to the live studio of the Good Morning, USA show. Jack saw it was the typical morning show set—everyday American living room, comfortable couch and chair, typical coffee table, two half-million-dollar-a-year anchor-persons. One of them, an ex-Miss America in glasses herself, smiled into the camera, "In just a few moments, we will be taking you live to the operating room of Metrocare Hospital to witness eye surgery history in the making. World-famous Dr. David Royster will be performing the first laser Free Electron Refractive Keratectomy on a patient to eliminate her nearsightedness. Dr. Royster had this to say earlier."

A closeup of Royster's face appeared on the screen. "Until today, millions of people all over the world would have to resort to glasses, contact lenses, or unpredictable surgery to correct their nearsightedness. The FERK electron laser has been developed in the USA, Japan, and Russia to reshape the cornea of the eye to change the nearsighted eye to a 20/20 eye without glasses. It is safe and performed in just a few seconds."

The anchorwoman reappeared, "And in just a few seconds we will be back to show that operation live. But first, this message." The instant lawn mower commercial appeared on the screen, the director came back on the audio. "Beautiful, beautiful. All right, we've just been introduced coast to coast. Is everyone set?".

"All set," said Royster.

"Set, hi," said Nakamura.

"Set," said Vorov.

"All crew in position and ready," said the stage manager, himself in a headset and down on one knee in the corner of the suite.

"Everyone on their toes," said the director. "We are now…" The commercial ended, "…live! Give me music and Camera 1."

The rumbling bass line of Thus Spake Zarathustra began, and the "Air" screen in front of the producer, all of the screens in the Surgery

Conference Theatre, and Jack's Number 1 monitor showed Maria in position on the Myogoround.

The narration began. "Today, here at Metrocare Hospital in New York City, we are about to witness the first laser operation for myopia performed in the world on a normal myopic patient. Before you stands the new Myogoround…"

The director spoke. "All right gentleman, that's our cue. Start the apparatus and the countdown."

Vorov pressed the activation button. As the computer began 120 seconds, 119, 118…," the stabilizer vacuum pulled Maria's head, arms, and legs tight to the conveyor seat, and her slow ascent on the conveyor loop towards the awaiting Royster began.

Out of the corner of his eye, Jack saw some commotion on his second monitor which showed Craig and the others in the observation chamber. He looked over, and saw what he'd expected—Dr. Matthews had arrived, out of breath, and was talking frantically to Miss Craig. The moment she understood, she, Matthews, and Crantz raced from the chamber, leaving a puzzled Miss Gutkopf and the medical students behind. Jack knew exactly where they were headed—to the stairs leading from the eye suite observation chamber to the one overlooking his.

"What gives in the observation chamber?" wondered Charlie.

The director ignored it. "Beautiful, beautiful," he said as Maria's body reached the crest of its ascent.

"…105, 104, 103…,"

Maria began to descend. Finally, as she reached the level of the FERK treatment platform, the seat unfolded into a stretcher on perfect cue, and Maria was slowly slid into position under the free-electron beam emitter.

The narration continued, "…automatically placing the patient into position for the treatment. Now you see the FERK machine itself, the device which holds the key to eliminating myopia in millions of people worldwide."

"Housekey. Key! Sam!" exclaimed Jack. "Key! Housekey! That must be it! I had forgotten completely. Mrs. Guardino said there was a house-key to unlock the data!"

Bankert was busy drawing up the milky white Deprivan solution into a syringe for Gabe's IV. "Whatever, Jack. I just work here."

Jack reached over and programmed in the connection to the Surgery Conference Theatre control room. He had to be cryptic. The director was on the same channel. "Charlie, this is your eye doctor again."

"That you doc?" responded Charlie promptly.

"You bet. Charlie. Try it again. Is the cursor still on the Myopia file?"

"Yep."

The director jerked his head up. "Who else is on the channel? What's going on? Is this in the script?"

Jack had to ignore him. "Charlie, we have to find another key. It unlocks the program. Understand?"

The director sounded slightly relieved. "I know. I know. It's the key to eliminating myopia. It's right in the script." Two other control room engineers in headphones looked around in bewilderment.

"Charlie," said Jack, overcoming his urge to whisper. "What would be a housekey on the computer?"

"'Escape' key maybe?"

"No, 'Escape' let's us out. We want something that let's us in."

"Press 'Control?' or 'Alt?'"

"No, no, not those. What else?"

"Let's see. Let's see. 'Delete? Press the 'Delete' key?"

The director joined in again. "Hurry up, Charlie, whatever you're doing. We're live, baby. No time for shop talk."

"Let's see, doc. 'Escape,' 'Control,' 'Alt,' 'Delete.' None of those. Let's see...,"

Jack and Bankert looked up at the suite monitor and watched Royster shift Maria's head several millimeters to bring her eyes directly beneath the red HeNe aiming beams. The optical scanner hummed, registering the retinal reflex. The countdown had just passed 90 seconds, "…88, 87, 86…,"

The first part of the narration ended with perfect timing. "…and now we see the patient in perfect alignment for the treatment as the machine itself goes into its automatic mode and countdown. We can hear the FERK doctors making their final checks."

"Everything fine here," said Royster over his headset. "Nakamura? Is the firing profile all set?"

A stream of Japanese followed, then, "All set," came the translated answer. "Patient's optical deficiency error 4 amd 5 diopters of myopia. Intended reduction 3.5 and 4.5 diopters. Treatment will have 20 bursts per second."

"Beautiful, beautiful," came the whispered coaching from the director. "We're going to win an EMMY. Alright, give me Camera 2 now, and at thirty seconds pre-firing let's start to roll that data and get that second part of the narration…"

Charlie came back on Jack's channel, "Gee, I'm out of ideas, doc. Except one key."

"What key? What's that?" Jack asked.

"The 'Home' key."

"Home?" exclaimed Jack. "Home? Why didn't you try it before?"

"C'mon, Jack. That's your number 7 key. I have the Num Lock on."

"The Num Lock! Charlie! That's it! The housekey is the 'Home" key. Seven was actually the 'Home" key. Quick! Unlock the Num Lock, press "Shift," and then hit "Home!" Hit home, Charlie! Hit it!"

There was a pause. Then, "Amazing doc. Absolutely amazing." Charlie sounded in awe.

"What is it, Charlie?" Jack demanded. "What happened?"

Charlie was watching the screen flashing and merging alphanumeric data faster than the eye could follow. "It's incredible, doc. I hit 'Home," and it's like this whole program is running on its own. It's the merge all right. Yep, it's merging just like you said."

The director, searching wildly among the video monitors for some explanation for the conversation, growled. "What's going on here? I want everybody doing exactly what they're supposed to."

Jack knew he had what he needed. "Great, Charlie, let it run! Thanks." Jack disconnected from the control room and let out a whoop.

"What was that all about?" asked Bankert, taping down Gabe's nasal oxygen cannula.

"'Home!' It was 'Home' all along, Sam!"

Bankert started to hum "Home On the Range," when there was a sudden pounding from above. Jack knew it would come. He looked up. There in the observation chamber, their noses pressed against the glass panels, were Miss Craig, Dr. Matthews, and Crantz. Matthews rapped feverishly on the glass. They were all obviously yelling, but through the thick panes their cries came faintly. Jack ignored them as he drew up a syringe of Xylocaine for Gabe's eye.

Suddenly the speakers in Jack suite blasted with sound. It was Miss Craig, screaming at the top of her lungs into one of the observation chamber's intercom microphones.

"Dr. Stegall! Stop this immediately! If you do not stop, we will be forced to come down there and break through the door. Dr. Stegall, stop it this instant!".

The countdown could still be heard over Miss Craig's voice. "...77, 76, 75...,"

"Stop it—stop it...! Her words were a chant. "Stop it—stop it...! Matthews and Crantz began to chant with her.

"Looks like the good lady and her friends are trying to blast us out of here," said Bankert, slowly injecting the Depri-van into Gabe's IV.

Jack flicked the syringe for bubbles and injected the numbing Xylocaine an inch from Gabe's right eye. "Sam, turn up the volume in the speakers up there to the max and give them a selection from your sound machine."

"You give me an idea, Jack. Steppenwolf- 1969—Magic Carpet Ride—coming up."

Bankert programmed from his keyboard. Moments later, the sounds of the Steppenwolf hit filled the suite and the observation chamber above, the introductory gradual crescendo of shrieking fuzz guitar and reverberating synthesizer growing to a deafening, throbbing frenzy. Bankert turned the operating suite speakers down to soft, but the observation chamber speakers up to maximal volume. The observation glass shook when the lyric began, "I like to dream! Right between the sound machine...!"

Exchanging panic-stricken looks and covering their ears against the deafening noise, Matthews and Crantz fled, but Craig remained and continued to rap on the glass with a metallic clipboard. "Stop it," she shrieked into the microphone. "Stop it!"

"She'll give up," encouraged Bankert. "I'm all set here, Jack. Better get started."

Jack slipped into the gown held out for him by Cissy, but when she extended the first surgical glove for Jack's right hand,

Craig's voice turned low and threatening. "Drop it, Cissy! I mean now!"

Cissy looked up at Craig and back at Jack. "I don't know, Dr. Stegall. Maybe..."

"Cissy!" shouted Craig. "Put that glove on and you'll be on a plane back to Jamaica!"

Cissy slowly looked up at Craig. Then she reopened the elastic glove, popping it for emphasis, and Jack plunged his hand into it. The left glove followed. "Thanks, Cissy," said Jack.

At the sight of Jack fully masked, gowned, and gloved, Craig howled and ran from the chamber.

Jack looked up at the monitor, and heard the FERK countdown pass the fifty second mark. "Sam, is Stravinsky's Le Sacre du Printemps on MegaMOM?"

"Affirmative."

"Key up the middle of the last movement and bounce it to override whatever music is programmed out of the SCT. Got it?"

"No prob." Bankert programmed it one-handed. "All set, Jack. Say when."

Jack heard the director give the cue for the Mozart Clarinet Concerto.

"Now, Sam, now."

Bankert hit the "Alt" key, and, after the first measure, the Mozart was abruptly replaced by the jolting staccato of the Stravinsky Danse Chorale (L'elue)—in the control room, SCT, and Royster's eye suite.

The director looked wildly about the control room. "What the hell—what happened to the music! What happened to the Mozart, Charlie?"

"Don't know, don't know!" Charlie was madly flipping dials and throwing levers. "Some short-circuit in MegaMOM. I can't get the music off!"

The director cursed. "Hell with it. Let it play."

"But—that's Stravinsky, I mean, The Sacrificial Dance, The Chosen Victim…"

The director's mind was elsewhere. "Never mind. Keep going. Stick to the script, everybody!"

Royster's voice came on. "What's that music? Where's my Mozart?"

Vorov chimed in. "Stravinsky. Vesna svyashchennaya. That Stravinsky."

"It's OK, it's OK, doctors, some snag," answered the director. "Ignore it. Watch the countdown."

Jack had heard it all as he watched the monitor showing the Royster suite. "OK, Sam, now give me an audio connection with the eye suite."

The anesthesiologist keyed in the command. "You're on the air in the eye suite. You do get around, my friend."

Jack watched Maria's face on his monitor as he spoke into his headset, "Maria! Maria Sanchez! You must listen carefully!"

Everyone in Royster's FERK suite jerked their heads up except Maria, who, immobilized by the restraining vacuum, only shifted her eyes to the right.

"This is Dr. Jack Stegall speaking, Gabe's friend. You must listen carefully! The FERK procedure is not safe! Repeat, it is not safe! The research data has been tampered with! There is clear danger of corneal scarring, and there may be another hidden complication! Maria, ignore what they tell you! Leave the OR suite!"

Maria looked frantically at Royster, who was glaring up at the ceiling-mounted loudspeakers.

"Get—him—off!" Royster fumed. "And get that—music off!"

"What?" Charlie and the director chorused. "Who?"

Jack had made sure his voice was transmitted only to the eye suite.

Royster jumped up, walked to Maria's side, kneeled, and spoke to her softly. "Maria, listen very carefully to me."

The director interrupted over the audio. "Dr. Royster. This is not in the script. I mean, it's very beautiful, you know, but what—the—hell—is—going on here?"

"A minor hitch," Royster spoke into his mouth mike. "The count-down will continue. I just have to tell the patient something."

"Cool, cool," said the director. "OK, OK, everybody keep their positions, keep on cue. Keep Royster's audio off the air."

"…42, 41, 40…,"

Royster leaned close to Maria's ear when the Stravinsky exploded into another frenzy of staccato and tympani. "Get it off," Royster raged at the ceiling. "Maria, this procedure is absolutely foolproof. And three, millions of television viewers are waiting to see this miraculous discovery performed. I know that you have the strength of character to proceed as our patient."

Maria looked at Royster, then at Nakamura, then back at Royster. "What happened? Why did Dr. Stegall…?"

"Trust me. There are reasons, unrelated to us and FERK."

Maria nervously nodded. Royster patted her shoulder and returned to his firing position. "We're now going into ready position, Maria." With a slow whir the firing sphere lowered, bringing the free-electron beam emitter within inches of her eyes.

CHAPTER *Twenty-eight*

Jack had watched it all on the central monitor, heard everything Royster had told her. It was no surprise. Now he had to depend on the data. Looking back and forth from the right monitor's camera view of Royster's suite and the left monitor's video feed going to Good Morning, USA, he waited until the countdown hit "35," then gave the computer its final instruction: to relay the airing of the data from the narrator's console exclusively to the eye suite. The control room monitors, the monitors in front of the audience in the surgery conference theater, and the feed to the studio would receive nothing of the data.

"...33, 32, 31...,"

At 30 seconds, the merged data began to stream across the bottom of the narrator's screen in the sound booth. Taking his cue, the narrator began, "The FERK procedure has been tested and proven in a surgical trial involving dozens of volunteers. Case after case has shown amazing results, as shown here..."

The data slowly streamed from right to left, and the narrator read verbatim. "Case number one, clear cornea. Case number two, poor healing, hazy, scarred corneas, and cataracts. Case number three, poor healing, hazy, scarred corneas, and cataracts..."

Everyone in the eye room froze. Royster stared at the monitor. Maria rolled her eyes sideways to watch the monitor. Nakamura looked up from his position at FERK controls. Vorov, standing next to the Myogoround, looked about in astonishent.

In Gabe's suite, Jack, Sam, and Cissy stared at their monitor.

"Cataracts?" asked Sam.

Jack nodded. "That was it, Sam. Cataracts. That was the other complication they were hiding."

The data and the narration continued. "...case number five, poor healing, hazy, scarred corneas and cataracts, case number six, poor healing, hazy, scarred corneas, and cataracts..."

"...24, 23, 22...,"

"What the hell is going on, what the hell is going on?" whispered the director. "And what the hell happened to the data?"

"Don't know," said a perplexed Charlie, looking back into the sound studio. "It's on the narrator's screen, and apparently it's going to the eye suite, but nowhere else. Some kind of override somewhere."

"OK. OK. No big deal," said the director. "It's not essential for the..."

Suddenly, Royster barked into his headset. "Turn it off!"

The director turned to Charlie frantically. "What does he mean, turn it off?"

"Turn it off! Turn off the data!" Royster's voice rose.

The director looked totally confused. "Charlie, he wants us to turn off the data, to stop the narration!"

Charlie stammered, "But that is the data. I mean, that's Royster's data, right?"

The data continued to be aired in Royster's suite. "Case number 11, hazy corneas with marked scarring and..."

"...18, 17, 16...,"

Royster leaped from his seat, jumped up on a stool and yelled into the wide-angled robotic camera. "Stop the data! Do you hear me! Stop that goddamned data!"

"Gimme Camera 2! Gimme Camera 2!" yelled the director to get Royster off-camera. "Dr. Royster, please. It's beautiful, but..."

"Stop the data!" Royster was now shaking his fists in the air.

"Cut!" screamed the director. "I mean, scramble the feed to the studio! Go to commercial! What the hell is going on around here?"

Instantly the "Air" monitor switched to the Good Morning, USA studio, where the anchorwoman had just heard the command. "Well, it looks like there is some kind of technical malfunction at Metrocare. Uh, just a moment." She paused to listen to her earphone. "Yes, we have a holdup on the operation. Don't go away, folks. And now this message from the makers of Dynasoap." The program switched to the commercial, eliciting a buzz of gasps and complaints from the audience in the Surgical Conference

Theatre. Several foreign reporters stood and looked back in the direction of the control room for an explanation.

"Hold on, everybody," said Charlie over the PA system. "Some kind of a blooper somewhere."

In the eye suite the data continued. Vorov, receiving the Russian translation of the data through his interpreter, looked over at Royster with surprise. Nakamura glared at his interpreters who were arguing in Japanese over the meaning.

"Blast it to hell," howled Royster. He reached up, yanked the cable from the closest monitor, and the screen went blank.

"12…"

"11…"

Royster leapt from the stool back to his firing position at the beam emitter hovering above Maria's eyes. "All right," he growled, "Everyone get set."

"Ten…"

The laser assumed a high pitched whine, "Ready to Discharge" warning lights began to flash, and the three doctors leaned forward in their positions in preparation to fire.

But a look of realization had come upon Maria's face.

"No!" she screamed. "Let me go!" She tried to sit up, but her torso and head remained vacuumed to the platform as if glued. "My god!" she cried. She raised her legs high in the air, and, kicking forward, lunged upwards, breaking the vacuum to a loud sucking pop—"Schhwopp"—and slid off of the operating platform. Royster lunged forward to push her back on. She dodged his grasp, and jumped to the other side, close to Nakamura.

"Get her, Nakamura," yelled Royster. "Get her back on. Nurses! Set up the IV! Get the anesthesiologist! Sedate her!"

Nakamura sprang at Maria, but stopped short when she assumed a karate position. The nurses gasped, dropped the IV tubing, and fled the room with a shriek.

"Obey!" barked Nakamura. When he reached out to catch her, she stepped forward and struck him in the mid-section with her left fist, doubling him over in agony.

"Get her Vorov!" bawled Royster. Vorov stepped forward, but when she jabbed twice, missing his nose by inches, he backed off to freeze against the wall next to the three interpreters and a cameraman who stood there panic-stricken.

Royster jumped up and moved towards Maria, but looked back as the countdown ran out.

"Three..."

"Two..."

"One..."

"Discharge!" The machine shuddered and fired its photonizing beam directly at the plastic head rest previously occupied by Maria's head, sizzling two deep holes from which thick, orangy-green plumes of vaporized plastic rose into the air and mushroomed across the ceiling.

Maria ducked to the left and ran out the side door, with Royster one step behind. As she turned into the corridor, she tripped over a wheel of the Myogoround, and he caught her arm and spun her around. "Come back in, do you hear!" he screamed through his mask into her face.

"Let go!" Maria wrenched free of his grasp, backed up, and went to a low crouch. When Royster stepped forward to grab her, she whirled full circle, striking him squarely in the nose beneath his mask with a perfectly executed roundhouse kick. Royster hurtled back, slammed into the side of the Myogoround, and crumpled to the ground, mask ripped to the side and nose bleeding profusely.

Nakamura and Vorov appeared, both shaken and panting for air. Vorov helped Royster to his feet, but Nakamura refused any assistance.

"What's wrong, Nakamura?" sputtered Royster, wiping his bloody nose with the sleeve of his surgical gown.

The Japanese doctor barked, "Bujoku Shiteiru!" and stomped away down the corridor in the direction of the surgeon's locker room.

"What was it?" Royster demanded of the Japanese interpreter.

"The doctor says he has been dishonored," came the terse answer.

"Dishonored?" wailed Royster. "It's his damned machine. You Japanese made it!"

The interpreter, looking just as offended as Nakamura, marched away.

"Wait! cried Royster. "I didn't mean…" Scrambling to his feet, he took off down the corridor in pursuit, Vorov following, with the remaining interpreters, cameramen, and Miss Gutkopf scurrying afterwards.

By this time, Maria was far down the corridor when one of her fellow medical students ran up to her with a hospital robe. "Oh my god, Maria! Do you know about Gabe?"

"No, what?" Maria swung into the robe.

"It's crazy. She's in neurosurgery! She was knocked out last night trying to get here to you! Dr. Stegall hijacked the operation. You'll see, come on!"

Both students raced back down the corridor and up the access stairs to the observation chamber above Jack's OR. As they entered, Jack looked up, waved at Maria, and returned to his work.

"All set, Sam?"

"All set."

"Hey, look Sam," said Jack, peering up at the monitor showing the Surgery Conference Theatre. "All our friends have wound up in the theater to watch us from there." Indeed, standing in the back, unnoticed by the confused reporters and visitors, were Craig, Matthews, and Crantz, looking on mutely with pale, haggard expressions.

"Let's give them a split screen to make it easy," said Bankert. He keyed in, creating a split view—half a wide shot of the operation, the other half the microscope image of Gabe's pupil.

Jack painted Gabe's upper right face with sterilizing solution and finished positioning the eye drapes. He felt his mask dampen with perspiration, and his hands were beginning to shake.

"Oops. Jack, look," said Sam. "Trouble again. Looks like some engineers have come to solve the little problem of our stuck door."

Jack looked over through the rectangular window. Three building engineers had arrived with a blow torch, and were setting up their gear in preparation to carve their way in. "Sam, no time to cut down. I'll have to aspirate with a syringe. Right now."

"Go for it."

Turning to the instrument tray, Cissy found a large syringe and 18 gauge needle and handed them to Jack. Hands trembling, Jack felt the lateral orbital rim with his forefinger, and pierced in next to it with the needle. He could feel it slide beside the eye, into the retrobulbar space. Bankert stood up to watch, then looked at the monitor. The pupil was still mid-dilated. Bankert zoomed in the overhead camera to show only Jack's syringe.

Jack pulled back on the plunger. Nothing came up. He removed the needle. "It may be semiclotted, Cissy. I need a bigger bore." Jack stepped to the instrument table, where Cissy exchanged the 18 with a size larger.

Bankert glanced over through the window. "Jack, last chance. Those guys out there are just about to light that blowtorch, and they'll have that door open pronto."

Jack returned to Gabe's side. Once again he pushed the needle in, this time going deeper. He pulled back slightly, gently. Nothing. He looked at Gabe's pupil, first directly, then on the monitor.

It was Bankert who first saw the trickle of semi-clotted blood into the syringe. "There it is, Jack! There it is!"

Jack had never released the vacuum entirely on the syringe plunger. He looked down. Blood slowly filled the plastic cylinder.

"Come on, come on!" coaxed Jack. He resisted an impulse to probe with the needle. He knew he was in the pocket, and the blood would come out gradually.

In the Surgical Conference Theatre, all of twelve screens carried only the images from Jack's operation. It was a medical student in the back row who first saw the blood filling the syringe. "Look. He's got it!"

"Shutup," barked Matthews from the back. "A lot of eye trauma has blood there. But the pupil is still dilated." He glared at the medical student.

"That's not correct, doctor." Half of the audience in the theater turned in the direction of the speaker sitting at the end of the front row. It was Dr. Koskey, Chief of the Columbia Eye Department. He stood up and silently pointed to a side monitor with a closeup of the eye.

The pupil was growing smaller.

Jack, his eyes riveted to his own monitor, counted aloud the decrease in the diameter of the pupil. "6 millimeters, 5, 4…" Finally he withdrew the needle, swung the microscope aside, withdrew the eye drape, placed some eye ointment into Gabe's eye, and applied a firm pressure dressing. It was only then that the tide of feelings—exhilaration, relief, anger, and fear of the consequences of his actions—washed over him. "All done here, Sam," he said hoarsely. He felt weak in the legs, and for a moment had to lean on the operating table for support.

Dr. Bankert removed the nasal oxygen, and disconnected Gabe from the monitors. Cissy went to the door, dislodged the cane, and opened it. The engineers stood up, blow torch yet unlit in their hands, perplexed.

"It's OK guys," smiled Cissy. "Dr. Stegall is through now. He just needed some privacy to spare this young lady from one of those unnecessary brain surgeries. Someone grab us a stretcher, OK?"

Two onlooking security guards fetched the gurney and rolled it over to Cissy at the open door.

Gabe groaned.

"Jack," said Bankert, checking Gabe's reflexes. "Looks like she's coming out of it some."

Jack touched her shoulder. "Gabe, it's Jack."

Gabe wearily opened her left eye and recognized him. "What happened? Jack, where am I? What...?"

"You were knocked out, hit in the right eye. I had to operate. You're going to be fine."

"Maria? What about Maria?" she said hazily.

Bankert answered. "Let's say she elected against the FERK operation at the last moment."

A tapping sounded from above. It was Maria, smiling and waving from the observation chamber. Gabe caught a glimpse of her before drifting off. Again Bankert checked her reflexes.

Jack looked at Sam worriedly. "What do you think?"

"I'm afraid she's drifting in and out. We just won't know how she'll end up for a bit. We'll just have to wait, Jack. I'll order a neurology consult right away."

"We're ready to take her to recovery now, doctors," said Cissy, adjusting Gabe's blanket.

They lifted her from the table to the stretcher and, Jack in the lead, Bankert and Cissy behind, wheeled her slowly from the suite, down the passageway, and into the main OR corridor. There they passed the gauntlet of flabbergasted onlookers who had flocked there from the Surgical Conference Theatre. Closest were Charlie, the TV director, Dr. Koskey, a half dozen medical students, and a half dozen reporters. A crowd of nurses, orderlies, and security guards took up the rear. Crantz, Craig, and Matthews were nowhere in sight.

"Nice going," said one of the medical students. Another student started to applaud, a third joined in, and finally everyone was softly applauding. Jack led the way past them towards the Post Anesthesia Care Unit until he was met by a small group of men led by the Chairman of the Hospital Board of Trustees, a tall, white-haired gentleman named Mr. William Edgerton, who officiously stepped forward.

"Dr. Stegall, I have been in contact with a quorum of the Hospital Board," he said. "We expect you in the Board Room, along with Drs. Matthews and Royster, and Mr. Crantz, in one hour." Edgerton sniffed, turned, and the group walked away.

CHAPTER *Twenty-nine*

When Jack arrived outside of the board room, Crantz and Matthews were already seated, looking drained and nervous. Royster was absent. Nobody spoke.

The board room door opened and the three men were escorted inside and directed to sit at the end of the long mahogony conference table. At the opposite end sat seven unsmiling men. Edgerton sat in the highbacked Chairman's seat. The Chairman of the Medical Executive Board, a veteran obstetrician named Dr. Malcolm Price, was positioned to his right, the hospital attorney to his left. Jack assumed the others were trustees. Behind them on the walls hung the obligatory gilt-framed oil portraits of former hospital chiefs and benefactors.

Sitting off to the side were Dr. Koskey and, next to him, Dr. Ed Baker. Baker, who smiled at Jack and raised his hand in an abbreviated sign of welcome, seemed the only one at that end of the room uninclined to throw anybody remotely culpable to the wolves. Next to Baker sat a poker-faced secretary taking minutes.

Edgerton rose to speak. "Gentlemen, this meeting will be very brief, for the purpose of informing you of what we have already learned about the circumstances surrounding the shocking events in the operating room this morning, and to tell you what further actions will be taken. Let me say at the outset that in my 20 years as a trustee of this hospital, I have never witnessed anything as extraordinary, as outlandish, as extreme as these events I witnessed from the Surgery Conference Theatre."

Matthews fidgeted in his chair and loosened his collar. Crantz, appearing nauseous, was busy with his handkerchief. But Jack, even to his own surprise, sat cooly in his seat, afraid of no one, not even of the pious patrician Edgerton.

Edgerton donned his reading glasses and pointed to one of several files laying before him. "We have fortunately been able to contact Dr. Giardano's widow and have confirmed that the data which was displayed in the eye suite this morning was indeed valid data which had been concealed. The data includes not only severe corneal scarring but also advanced cataract formation. It appears that Dr. Royster masterminded this fraud, then deceived and pressured Dr. Giardano into cooperating." The chairman looked about the room irritatedly. "Where is that Royster? He is supposed to be here."

Baker jumped up and went to the wall phone to put out the call for the absentee.

Edgerton continued. "If it were not for the actions of Dr. Stegall, the fraud would have culminated in the FERK operation being imposed upon God knows how many unsuspecting people, starting with one of our medical students right here in our own hospital. At the same time, Dr. Stegall, your exposure of this heinous scheme was itself almost telecast city and nationwide, not to mention being publicized in every major newspaper in the world. The damage to the reputation of our fine hospital would have been immeasurable." He glared at Jack, but Jack didn't flinch. "Uh, fortunately, this did not come to pass," Edgerton stammered. "I have been assured that this ugly situation has been contained within these walls, and we are in a position to handle the entire matter internally."

He picked up a second file and spoke directly to the other trustees. "Now, on the subject of Dr. Stegall's commandeering of the neurosurgery operative suite. From the information available to us at this time, it appears that Stegall did perform the indicated operation, but..."

Dr. Matthews started to interrupt.

"Dr. Matthews, if you don't mind," scolded Edgerton. "As I was saying, it appears that Dr. Stegall did perform the indicated operation, but had no authority to do so. Operating without appropriate authority is a serious offense."

"Mr. Chairman, may I speak?" It was Dr. Koskey who interrupted. "I realize that I have been invited to this meeting ex- officio, but our medical student who had volunteered for the FERK operation, Miss Sanchez, spoke with me a few minutes ago about the circumstances leading up to the operation. I understand that the neurosurgeon's decision to perform a craniotomy was based on the consultative diagnosis of the eye resident, one Dr. Arnsdorf, is that correct?"

"I believe so, yes that is correct," answered Dr. Price. Matthews said nothing.

Koskey paused to listen to something Baker was whispering to him, then went on. "I also understand that although the resident conferred with Royster, who was out of the hospital—at the Plaza, I understand—and concurred with his diagnosis, that Royster never saw the patient, and never co-signed the resident's note in patient Richard's chart."

"I have her chart right here. Let's see," said Dr. Price, flipping to the doctor's notes. "Yes, that is correct. But I'm not sure of your point, Dr. Koskey. Attending physicians sign off on resident's decisions all the time, especially under emergency situations."

Koskey smiled. "I agree. But in this situation, over 8 hours passed before the operation was scheduled, plenty of time for Dr. Royster to have seen the patient, examined her, and co-signed the resident's note, if not make a note of his own. I think it is clear that this was not an emergency in a crisis sense. Now, up at our Medical Center, the by-laws state that when there is no co-evaluation and co-signing by the consultant, that for all intents and purposes, the consultation is rendered invalid and void."

"OK, but where does that get us?" stammered Edgerton.

Koskey held his palms out. "I would propose to you that this is an extenuating circumstance. Dr. Stegall may not have had the authority to operate, but neither did Dr. Matthews. Matthews never did have a valid authorization to operate after 8 hours had passed."

"True," said Dr. Price, closing Gabe's chart. "But neither did Stegall have any authority to operate, even if Matthews didn't."

"Then just who the hell did have the authority?" growled Edgerton.

Dr. Baker spoke up. "Excuse me, but it would be the ophthalmologist on call at the time of the operation."

"Damn it, who was that?" sputtered the Chairman.

Baker opened his briefcase and took out the On Call Schedule. "Dr. Royster's call ended at 8 a.m. The next ophthalmology attending was—let's see." He turned to the next page. "Dr. Giardano."

Edgerton rolled his eyes. "But Dr. Giardano expired two days ago. Who takes his place?"

Baker answered. "Incapacitation of a physician on call? The next doctor in the rotation fills in. Let's see, that doctor would be...," He turned to a third page, then looked over at Jack and smiled. "Gentleman, Dr. Stegall was officially on call."

Looks of surprise swept the room.

"Well I'll be damned," said Dr. Price.

"All right, all right," said Edgerton. "So, gentlemen, these are the facts as we know them at this time. Now, certain actions are in order. Mr. Crantz, we have learned, and you have acknowledged, that you had prior knowledge of the manipulation of the data before the operation this morning. Mr. Crantz, your duties as Administrator for this hospital are herewith summarily suspended, and you will be placed on administrative leave. You will be notifed as to further actions, but frankly I think you should start to look seriously for employment elsewhere. You are excused."

White-faced and speechless, Crantz got up and left.

Edgerton looked directly at Jack. "Dr. Stegall, at the start of this meeting, I was prepared to suspend your activities as an eye surgeon here at Metrocare pending further investigation. However, it appears…"

He was cut short when the door banged open and an incensed Royster stomped into the room. He had changed into a gray business suit, and wore a slightly bloodied sponge bandage inside his left nostril.

"So good of you to join us," said Edgerton icily. "Please take a seat. We will attend to you in a minute."

Royster took a chair next to one of the trustees, folded his arms, and stared at the opposite wall.

"As I was saying, Dr. Stegall," Edgerton continued. "It appears that although your methods were extreme, your actions were successful, and you have not violated the by-laws of the institution. You remain in good standing as an active surgeon with full hospital privileges."

Edgerton looked at Jack as if expecting some kind of thank you. Jack said nothing, wondering to himself if the hospital neurologist evaluating Gabe would predict recovery or further deterioration.

"Dr. David Royster," Edgerton addressed him with open contempt, "It is now my duty to inform you that, according to the power invested in the Board of Trustess, you are summarily suspended from all activities at this hospital. May I advise you that your very next step should be to retain the services of an exceptional attorney. It will be our duty to report what appears to be gross scientific fraud to numerous regulatory agencies, including the New York State Board of Medicine and the Federal Food and Drug Administration. Office space at Whittaker has the prerequisite of privileges at Metrocare. You will be given a suitable amount of time to make arrangements."

"And what exactly is that supposed to mean?" snapped Royster.

"It means you have to relocate your practice, doctor."

Everyone except Royster turned their head towards the speaker—it was Jack. Finally, slowly, Royster turned in his direction and scowled. "Stegall, you…!"

The smile forming on Jack's face was irrepressible.

Edgerton closed his files and slipped his glasses into his vest pocket. "This concludes this meeting, gentlemen. Good day."

Royster jumped to his feet, a look of molten rage on his face. "So! You think you can destroy me just like that. Well, let me tell you something, all of you. You don't scare me. Not for a minute. The FERK procedure does work. All great inventions have had their setbacks…."

Royster was interrupted when the door bumped open and a security guard strode in. "I have to find Dr. Edgerton," the guard said.

Edgerton motioned him over, and the guard handed him a note.

Edgerton read it silently, then looked over at Royster. "Dr. Royster, your troubles are much greater than I imagined. The police would like to speak with you out in the hallway."

CHAPTER *Thirty*

Three months later

Jack swung into the right hand lane to make the turn for Queens and LaGuardia Airport. As was the custom of many new medical school diplomates, a vacation was taken between graduation and the beginning of internship July 1st. Gabe had suggested the Bahamas, Jack, Bermuda. They settled on the Turks and Caicos. Jack handed the tickets to Gabe, and she confirmed the departure time. The American flight would leave at 2:35 p.m.

They were coming direct from the Columbia Presbyterian Medical Center where the graduation ceremonies had been held earlier in the day. Gabe—totally recovered from her head injury— had finished with honors. Jack had received the new faculty award, and had also been invited to speak. But it never came to pass.

The graduation scene was still fresh in his mind. He had been one of the last to take his place among the medical school deans and senior faculty seated on the long low platform facing the senior class. The medical students, numbering 156, solidly filled the front eight rows. Behind them sat parents and invited guests, flanked by several hundred junior faculty, lower class medical students, and well-wishers. Reaching under his academic gown, Jack patted the note card he had prepared for his speech.

The location, in the garden directly behind the main building of the Columbia Presbyterian Medical Center, had been the same for Jack when he had graduated 15 years before, and for countless classes before him. He had forgotten the occasion's colorful beauty: the flowing sky-blue and black academic robes, the tasseled mortar boards and tams, the azaleas and periwinkles exploding in white and pink along the paths and walkways, all set against a background of smooth lawns, grassy knolls, and what had turned out to be a flawless, sun-drenched afternoon. Gabe was sitting in the sixth row, and Maria was a few seats away.

After the diplomas had been awarded, the dean of the medical school offered his congratulations to the class, and then introduced the key speaker, an aging professor courageously recovering from a stroke, who held forth on "The New M.D.: Challenges of the Future." The speech, urging the new medical graduates to overcome adversity by adhering to moral principles, seemed almost identical to the oration that had inspired Jack at his graduation. To Jack, the lofty words seemed to contradict as much as inspire: surmount the insurmountable, endure the unendurable, be battered but come out whole. Jack's prepared remarks would offer a different, more down-to-earth point of view.

The Special Awards were presented first to the students, then to a handful of faculty. Jack's award was last. As the dean began his introduction, Jack felt suddenly nervous. Lectures on the eye were one thing. To be called upon to give guidance to 156 new physicians was another.

"Our final presentation," the dean said, repositioning the tassel on his mortar board, "is a new award established by a generous endowment from the family of the late Dr. Robert Giardano. The award goes to that faculty member who, by vote of the entire graduating class, has most exemplified those qualities of moral courage which are essential to the ethical practice of medicine. It is an honor to announce the first Robert Paul Giardano Award recipient: Dr. Jack Stegall."

To warm applause Jack rose and walked to the podium. He was reaching in his pocket for his notecard when the dean leaned close to whisper. "Dr. Stegall, I'm terribly sorry, but we're running over one hour behind. If you could just—I'm sure you understand…"

Jack had no choice but to accept his award, thank the class, and sit down.

They were crossing the Triborough Bridge when Gabe asked what happened.

"They ran out of time," he said.

She rolled up her window against a stiff East River breeze. "You have your notes with you. Can I see?"

"They're just an outline of my ideas. I was going to extemporize."

"I'd still like to read them."

Jack handed her the card.

"Let's see. It just says 'clipping, Pamela Wilcox letter, and John Wilcox E-mail.'"

Jack removed a newspaper clipping and two folded sheets from his coat pocket. "I was going to use these for excerpts."

Gabe unfolded the clipping and read it aloud:

"The New York Times—Dr. David Royster, a world-renowned eye surgeon, was sentenced to life imprisonment yesterday in a New York City Federal Court for the murder of Pamela Wilcox of Jersey City, New Jersey. Dr. Royster, the President and CEO of Globe, Inc., was found guilty of contracting for the murder of Ms. Wilcox with an escaped convict, Mr. Thomas "Bird" Blake. Mr. Blake, who had confessed to the murder in the face of incontrovertible DNA evidence, turned state's witness and testified against both Dr. Royster and his business associate, Ms. Helga Gutkopf. Ms. Gutkopf subsequently confessed to attempted murder as an accessory in a similar arrangement with Mr. Bird in a related case. Though Mr. Blake has been returned to a New York State Federal Prison, both he and Dr. Royster were charged last week with with the drowning murder of Mr. George Sutcliff, a Manhattan com-

puter engineer who was the founder of a website that was connected to
the case."

Gabe looked over at Jack. "They didn't mention the evidence—Bird's
DNA matching the skin under Pamela Wilcox's fingernails."

Jack shrugged. "Or Bird's blood they found in her stolen car when
they found it abandoned in the Bronx. I called the Times. They're going
to do an in-depth article next week."

Gabe unfolded the first letter. Jack glanced over. "It's a copy of the letter, the one they found in the manila envelope under the seat in her car."

Gabe read it aloud:

"Dear Dr. Giardano, I know nobody is perfect, including doctors. but
what I have seen at my hospital gives me no choice but to come to you
for help. I am nearsighted myself but I mainly went to work on an eye
ward because of what happened to my brother.

On the ward I saw dozens of homeless men coming through who had
the laser procedure at your hospital by one of your departmental colleagues, Dr. David Royster. All of them were almost blind. They were
too intimidated to talk about what had happened to them. I know
enough about the eyes to know that their corneas were completely
scarred. but what really shocked me was that an increasing number of
the men developed cataracts on top of the corneal scarring, and it was
all being covered up…"

"So she knew it was cataracts, the second complication Royster was
covering up," Gabe said.

Jack nodded, and Gabe continued to read Pamela Wilcox's letter:

"…I might have just looked the other way except for my younger
brother John. A few years ago he had the operations for his nearsightedness on both eyes. His vision was ruined

forever. He became very depressed. He told his story on the Internet on the web site 'lasereyes.com.' His name was John Wilcox, but he put his story under the initials John W. You can see in the last paragraph how depressed he was by what the doctors did to him. He took a shotgun and shot himself thru both eyes on New Years Eve. I just want to do everything I can to stop Dr. Royster from destroying more peoples' lives the way they detroyed my brothers. Sincerely yours, Pamela Wilcox, R.N."

"It gives me goose bumps," Gabe said. She unfolded the second page "And this is her brother's E-mail?"

Jack nodded as he passed a bus. "I printed it out from Lasereyes.com after they got it up and running again. There are thousands of people who are leaving similar messages."

Gabe unfolded the page and read:

"My name is John. I had radial keratotomy on my right eye two years ago and the the latest laser operation on my left one year ago. Before the procedures I could see fine with glasses or contacts. I just didn't like wearing them, and all the ads and my doctor said that their operations were miraculous and that complications were rare and temporary. A few of my friends had it and they seemed satisfied. And my doctor said in his TV ads that he did the procedure on some professional athletes and movie stars.

Ever since the operations my life has been pure hell. Now on anything less than a sunny day my vision is blurry. At all times I suffer severe eyestrain, headaches, eye fatigue, and blurred vision. At night there are debiliating halos and starbursts around lights and even watching TV is unpleasant. I can't read a computer screen. Driving at night is frightening and dangerous.

My original doctors and the dozens of doctors I have seen for relief just shake their heads and say that either they don't understand what happened or that I am a hypochondriac. I have been through over 50 pairs of glasses and contacts but nothing helps. I know for a fact there are thousands of people out there just like me. These doctors know what's going on, but they hide it. Nobody does anything, not even the doctors who don't do this surgery.

I have two beautiful kids and a wife that I have missed out on ever since the operations. My wife has to handle everything. I am unable to work. I've missed out on the holidays such as Christmas and the joy of my kids opening their presents. I missed out on school functions and plays and most of my kids softball and baseball games. I've lost tens of thousands of dollars in expenses and lost income. Also, my father came down with Parkinson's Disease last year, and I am unable to spend time with him. I used to love sports activities and exercising. I do none of this anymore.

I am basically a robot controlled by the pain and stress that I have every minute of the day because of my deformed corneas.

Not has only have these operations ruined my life, but the operations have deeply affected my family and everyone who loves me. My wife now takes medicine to control her depression. My children are not doing well in school. I've thought about suicide but I won't do it because I have too much to live for. But I have to admit the pain is becoming unbearable not only from my eyes but also from my life.

The human eye is a beautiful creation. I would not recommend cutting or lasering it except in eye conditions where the person has no choice. John W."

"What do you think?" Jack asked.

Gabe folded up the papers and leaned her head on Jack's shoulder. "That would have been some graduation speech."

THE END

Author's Afterword

Today a new, revolutionary operation to reduce nearsightedness, LASIK (Laser Assisted In Situ Keratomilieusis) grows in popularity by leaps and bounds. In this procedure, the anesthetized cornea (the clear window of the eye) is pressurized, shaved open, thinned internally with the ultraviolet radiation of an excimer laser, and resealed. The operation takes minutes, and costs approximately $2500 per eye.

The hundreds of thousands of people flocking to LASIK surgeons worldwide testify to the operation's high rate of success and safety, at least short-term. The vast majority of patients are satisfied with their reduced dependency on glasses and contact lenses, and recommend the procedure to relatives and friends.

However, complications do occur, some merely inconveniencing, e.g., small undercorrections, but others ruinously debilitating, including halos, streaks, ghost images, blurred vision, loss of contrast, poor night vision (many must give up night driving), double vision, dry eyes, and headaches. Though some of these serious complications may subside with time or be alleviated with reoperations, others are permanent.

The actual incidence and permanence of such disastrous LASIK complications is a subject of some controversy. Most LASIK surgeons espouse the belief that serious complications are, in the hands of highly-experienced surgeons, rare and almost always temporary or treatable. Some LASIK surgeons argue, despite the lack of evidence, that complications (infections) from contact lenses exceed those of LASIK. Recently, the United States Food and Drug Agency gave LASIK its stamp of approval, although a potentially significant number of patients in the clinical studies reviewed failed to return for followup examinations.

However, the small but steadily growing number of patients visually crippled by LASIK believe that, even with the "best" surgeon, the true incidence of serious complications is at least 1% if not considerably higher. Many of these distraught patients are coalescing into groups advocating full disclosure of this higher degree of risk to prospective patients. They believe that such disclosure, along with knowledge of the undisputed fact that long-term potential side-effects are unknown, would reduce the numbers choosing surgery to those few who have truly compelling, justifiable reasons to place themselves at risk.

Readers interested in learning more from this disabled patient minority group should click on "www.surgicaleyes.org" or search for similar websites. (Note: comparable websites for patients disabled by contact lens wear do not exist, indicative of the relatively low incidence and severity of contact lens wear complications).

The "free-electron laser" is an experimental laser currently used in research centers such as the University of Utah Laser Institute. It's use in BLIND AMBITION for the "FERK" procedure is fictitious.

Printed in the United States
2527

9 780595 151110